The Buddha of Ballyhuppahaun

A New Age Fable

BY JOHNNY RENKO

The Buddha of Ballyhuppahaun – A New Age Fable
by Johnny Renko

First Published in Ireland by WiredWithWhelan in 2010

ISBN 978-0-9566996-01

www.wiredwithwhelan.com
johnnyrenko@gmail.com

Printed by Print Central, Portlaoise
Designed by Penhouse Design
Drawings by Gemma Guihan
Cover Photography by John Whelan
Foreword by Prof Jim Whelan
Audio book narrated by Nick Anton
Edited by Darren O'Loughlin

This book is typeset in 12pt Garamond on 13pt
Printed on Munken Lynx Rough
Paper by Paper Assist, Ireland.
www.paperassist.ie

FSC

Recycled
Supporting responsible
use of forest resources

Cert no. TT-COC-003334
www.fsc.org
© 1996 Forest Stewardship Council

PEFC™

BMT-PEFC-0930

The paper used in this book comes from the wood pulp
of managed sustainable forests achieving FSC
and PEFC chain of custody certification.

Inspired by the Rainbow Travellers
who came to the Slieve Bloom Mountains
in the summer of 1993

For Grażyna
And our children
Faith, Ricky and Martyna

In gratitude for the blessing of such great friends
and a wonderful family

Foreword

One distinguishing feature of human beings is undoubtedly their awareness. They are keenly aware of themselves and others around them. This awareness extends beyond a mere physical recognition and involves a complex understanding of the society, world and universe they inhabit.

Furthermore, this awareness also extends to non-human life. The earth, with its abundance of diverse life forms, has been a central fascination for human beings right back to their emergence as a social species. Just look at the first drawing on cave walls, for example: it is man's interaction with nature that is depicted. Humans have always been rooted in nature and caring for nature has been a theme of every major culture. Indeed, this care and responsibility is a common bond between humans and it has crossed tribes, races and religions. Even in today's consumer society, there are few who actively think that destruction of nature is appropriate, as societies' great burdens are placed on our environment.

All life began in water. The substance is seemingly so abundant that we take it for granted; we expect endless amounts of clean, pure water to sustain our bodies and to wash away the grime we collect in our daily lives. We use it widely as a recreation resource. We expect (actually, *demand*) all this for free, and the protests that arise when we are asked to pay a single dollar per day for endless clean water can bring down governments. This is the case even if, as is commonplace, we are prepared to pay several dollars for a few hundred millilitres of water with a designer label (most likely one that has some added impurities).

The 'health' of water is a mirror for the health of all life on our planet. Too much gaseous water will result in the greenhouse effect and our planet will boil, while too much solid water will leave us in an ice age. Moreover, too-high quantities of liquid water can cause much of the landmasses where we live to become saturated with the stuff.

Although we are familiar with the concept of peak oil, could it be that we have reached peak clean water levels? Can we supply enough clean water to sustain life? Arguably not, as our waterways and seas are now so polluted that many forms of life that we claim to cherish are being pushed to extinction.

However, this is only the tip of that iceberg that is now clearly visible, but we ignore the obvious deterioration on our environment because of our blind faith in our ability to control nature. Already, changes in rainfall patterns are causing huge problems for processes that depend on water – the major one being agriculture, which consumes over 70 per cent of irrigated water.

It takes thousands of litres of water to produce 1kg of beef; that's tens to hundreds of times more water to produce the equivalent calorie source from plant sources alone. Along with the significant input of animal production into greenhouse gases (estimates range from 10 to 50 per cent of all emissions), combined with the environmental degradation that occurs in developed and developing countries, the production of animals for agriculture alone is having a devastating effect on our planet.

Despite this, in the next 50 years food production must double just to feed the growing global population, predicted to reach nine billion people. The world has, at best, a three- to six-month reserve of food supply, meaning that if food production stops for a few months, everyone is at the risk of starvation. Coupled with this, all our food production depends on adequate water falling in the right place and being available and essentially free for food production. Even relatively small changes in rainfall patterns that move rainfall away from agricultural areas can have large downstream effects.

If water becomes more obviously scarce, would it be at all surprising if some unscrupulous entrepreneur were to try to make money on it? What prospects would this then have for food costs? The combination of peak oil and limiting water, added to the pressures of a growing world population means that we will hit a perfect storm that will result in higher food prices in the coming months and years. This scenario is not even decades away.

'No', comes the usual reply, 'Nobody would allow that to happen'. Is that so? Some years ago, a tax on air was considered a joke. Now, a 'carbon' tax has become a reality, but who will pay for it? Not the people who are causing the problem and who have made endless billions polluting our other abundant resource – air.

This pollution will now cause changes in our climate and will result in enormous strains on all life on this planet, including our ability to simply feed ourselves. We can produce enough food to feed the world. Food production was – and can be again – a sustainable, profitable business, if carried out in an environmentally sustainable manner. However, it cannot be sustainable if it is to fund the food oligarchs, just as oil and other natural resources have in the past.

This book is a cautionary tale about why we need to engage and buy into what is happening around us. We need to see through the false prophets that tell us all is OK and that there is nothing to worry about. We need to take back what belongs to us all: free air, water and nature. This book presents this case in a diverse and rich cultural context, drawing in language, fables and traditions from around the world. All destruction of nature is a local and global problem. It is easy (and relatively inexpensive) to reverse the problem; it just requires that we *want* to do it.

The quote that reads, 'All that is necessary for the triumph of evil is for good men to do nothing' applies to us all on this one – we all need to choose a side now! You decide the outcome.

Professor Jim Whelan
University of Western Australia, Perth

Nature

There is a delight in the hardy life of the open
There are no words that can tell the hidden spirit of the wilderness that can
reveal its mystery, its melancholy and its charm
The nation behaves well if it treats the natural resources as assets which it must
turn over to the next generation increased and not impaired in value
Conservation means development as much as it does protection.

Theodore Roosevelt

CHAPTER I

The Courgette Beds

'Those were the days my friend,
We thought they'd never end.
We'd sing and dance,
Forever and a day.'

These were the days he liked best. The time and place where all the seasons flowed together. From Monicknew he could view across the plain to the Ridge of Capard, the brow of Ballycoolan and the Windy Gap. From here, he could see the ends of the earth. Everywhere in between was spring, summer, autumn and winter. He could never pick his favourite, no matter how often pressed by others and surrounded by excited eyes and ears, for they all had something special and a special place in his heart.

The Buddha was homeward bound again. Regardless of how far he travelled, he always came home. He had travelled not for miles or metres, not for days and nights, nor yet for years and decades or even centuries, as he was not used to measuring life and living in this way. He had travelled forever and a day. He had travelled to the end of time and back. He was the Buddha of Ballyhuppahaun, the enchanted place, and he was heading home. Home is where the heart is. 'Níl aon tinteán mar do thinteán féin': he had heard that one night by the raging fire in Kinnitty Castle, where he paid a visit to the Mighty Con. He had been hatching at the heart, so snug was the castle in the glow of the flames, the music as inebriating and liberating as life itself. Now his heart weighed heavy, and although weary, there was no time for hogging the hearth tonight. That dreamtime stuff would have to wait for now. The Buddha was on a mission.

Dodo was by the Buddha's side. A faithful friend, he seldom left the Buddha's shadow once he returned to the Slieve Blooms. They would have plenty of fun together now, as no matter how often they played out their ritual, it was always as exciting as if it were new and for the first time. There was a blanket of snow on the far brow of Fossey Mountain but exploring that would come later. For now, they were headed for Glenbarrow. The gigantic waterfall with its thunderous torrents dwarfed even the mighty cascades of Iguaçu. Dodo could already taste the spray and even though they were still two full days' walk away, he could catch a glimpse of the butterflies as they played in the early morning sun. Flapping and fluttering, the butterflies – billions of them – rivalled the rainbow in colour as they flirted from one side of the falls to the other. This is deadly, thought a delighted Dodo. Reading his mind, the Buddha smiled, slapped him on the back and, with a trademark click of his heels and flick of his feet, followed up with a gentle toe to Dodo's derriere as the two hurtled along, hungry to get to Glenbarrow, one of their favourite spots.

Buddha and Dodo had many such favourites – West Cork, Buzios, Donegal, Achill, Mazury, the Kakadu, Kimberley, the Cotes de Basques, Hendaye, Le Morne, Galicia, Connemara – and it was always hard to choose, not between places, but to put one feeling, one memory, above another. Sometimes just for fun they would try, but always landed back at the same spot, just as they knew they would, agreeing to disagree and concluding it was not possible to compare in the first place. The Buddha would deliver a belly laugh as he tired Dodo into submission, having knocked great sport out of the fantastic journey through their shared memories.

It was down across the Cut, the Festival Field, Slievenamon, Slieve Rua and around by Reary, Rosenallis, up the Glendine Gap, sometimes running, racing to beat the daybreak that signalled its approach with a gilt-edged glow silhouetting the Ridge of Capard. A hop, skip and jump across the Owenass River, Dodo slipping on the skittish surface of a limestone slab midstream, provoking yet another trademark chortle from the Buddha. On home ground the Buddha was solid, staff in hand and no slip-ups. He oozed confidence – and garlic from last week's welcome home feast – galore.

Along the bohereen that wriggled past the villages of Birr, Cadamstown, Kinnitty and Clonaslee they bolted, posies of primroses and cowslips hugging the tufts of grass fringes, blinding the moss-glazed stone walls. Where undergrowth lay thickly, they tunnelled down through the briar lane, re-working the old track they had worn there before, catching only frail thorns and glimpses of light through gaps in the holly, hazel and hawthorn hedges. Nearly there now. Well worth the effort, this will be.

To some surprise did they suddenly emerge over a final mound to meet the sunrise head-on. Here in the heart of the Slieve Bloom Mountains they squatted down by the source of the burling Barrow brown. Springing from the sandstone, it gushes sprightly through the plains, before engaging and gossiping with the Nore and the Suir, three sisters heading for the sea in the south.

Buddha and Dodo draw a breath on the edge of the pasture that unfolds along the valley. They have arrived with not a second to spare. What a sight, what a sight. The Buddha was bursting with satisfaction. Dodo would surely be pleased. Buddha had promised him something special and this would not disappoint. The headland was embroidered with bunches of buttercups and daisies but the sight to behold lay hemmed in between. The Courgette Beds were just awakening to the day's rays and as they did, their yellow flowers trumpeted the dawn, signalling the start of the latest crop, brilliant blossoms reflecting and daring the dazzling sun. Such an exhibition was seldom and short-lived, but for the much-travelled Buddha, remained one of the wonders of the world.

"Have you ever seen anything quite like that?" queried the Buddha, anticipating only one answer or, failing that, none, as amazement would suffice. Mindful of his place, the Dodo obliged and stayed silent.

"Short and sweet, like the ass's gallop," the Buddha added with a glint in his eye.

Still dazed by the spectacle of a carpet of yawning yellow flowers spread out before him, the Dodo could not hold out any longer. A stream of questions poured forth: What was the secret? Why did the flowers blossom so magnificently, only to perish in such a short time? Why did such stunning specimens shrivel so soon?

The Buddha had been expecting such an outpour. Dodo would mider you with questions and, hence, a conundrum would arise: To chide and chastise him now would be to forever curb his instinctive inquisitiveness, while to answer would only encourage an avalanche of further queries.

The Buddha reached for a wild rhubarb leaf and, in one fluid motion, folded it into a funnel and captured fresh water shooting out of the rock before it had time to land again. So refreshing was it that he repeated the process a few times over, deliberately letting some water sluice down his chin and chest. Dodo followed suit, as he too was parched from the Buddha's forced march.

"Right so," says the Buddha abruptly, "pick only the finest flowers, take as much as you want, but want as much as you take. Pick an extra portion lest we have a guest, but leave plenty for those who follow in our footprints. The rest is for nature. Remember, waste not, want not."

Dodo knew this sermon and ceremony off by heart but enjoyed it nonetheless. The Buddha may have had his failings, and the whispers of such were growing ever louder about, but you could not fault him on this commandment.

"Courgettes," Buddha continued, "the same and don't forget that 'biggest' is not always 'best'. They'll be too pasty and chewy like cardboard, but we want them ripe and juicy. Otherwise, we might as well graze like cows." Dodo wanted to ask just when had the Buddha tasted cardboard, but dared not push his luck.

The bell-shaped flowers would hold their form once picked and chilled. Stuffed and coated with tempura, they would make a tasty appetiser. Courgettes were the essential ingredient for fortitude in this main course, to help fuel the remainder of the ongoing journey.

"I don't know," spoke the Buddha, out of the blue. Stooped down over a show-stopping specimen, he directed himself towards Dodo, who was further down the field. "I don't know why the flowers blossom so magnificently but briefly."

Dodo listened, disappointed. After all this time, he thought, that's the best the Buddha could come up with: "I don't know." Pitiful. Perhaps people were right about the Buddha after all.

"I thought you were a wise one?" Dodo angrily enquired.

"Wise? Perhaps, who knows? Only time will tell, but will not tell us in time," countered Buddha.

"But after all the time and travel and teaching, I thought you would know all, Buddha," Dodo admitted with a searching look.

"Know all," echoed the Buddha, straightening up, brandishing two fistfuls of courgettes. "Know all," he bellowed out across the valley. "What a terrible affliction and state of mind that would be, to be a know-all. It is a wise man that knows what he doesn't know Dodo, knows what he doesn't know." Buddha repeated the crucial phrase, as was his habit — for effect —

when he was slightly aggravated. He was not annoyed with Dodo, rather with those who filled his head in such fashion.

The pair continued to potter around, compiling their cache. The courgette crop was central, while the rest of the ingredients the Buddha had lugged with him in his distinctive mála mór satchel. A 'man bag', he had heard it dubbed, on the way over Mount Mellick. Such audacity, he grumbled to himself, but never mind, he was not going to let it spoil his recipe for success.

Sliced courgettes with chopped onions and garlic clove, fried in butter. Some stock, coarse black pepper and rock salt to simmer. Stirred and blended by the Buddha with a splash of cream and cubed Dolcelatta cheese. Et voila! The Buddha's world-famous courgette and Dolcelatta soup, served with cuts of warm, crusty bread. Scrumptious.

Dodo, meanwhile, enjoyed these trysts with the Buddha and wasn't going to let up now: "They also say that a man in silent and pensive mood, keeping himself to himself, with little to say as he sips on his uisce beatha and sucks on his duidín, is in fact a wise man, more so than someone who is mouthing all of the time."

"Is that what they say? And who are 'they'?" The Buddha snapped, before quickly composing himself, totally realising and fully regretting his flush.

"In Bogtown," Dodo answered offhandedly.

"Bogtown," Buddha rejoined, no longer miffed. "The legendary tea boys and the lords of Bogtown and weile, weile, waile. That explains everything; now I do know all," he teased Dodo. "An empty tin can sitting silent in the corner is still an empty tin can. A thimble can be filled with a spit and a fool, sitting at a counter, drinking whiskey, smoking a pipe and with nothing to remark upon except the weather, remains a fool. A silent fool on a stool is still a fool. It could be that someone saying nothing simply has nothing to say. Those who have something worth saying should say it, or they too join forces with the fool."

"I will get the firewood for our feast," Dodo eventually proclaimed, the Buddha's diatribe ricocheting round his skull. Fools, stool, as stubborn as a mule, he sang inside his head, but did not risk not even whispering it aloud.

As he set about his sun salutations, the Buddha looked forward to his food. The mouth-watering anticipation reminded him vividly of the surfing roadtrips he so loved. When evening fell, there would be a disorientating medley of faces and names, hunkered round a roaring fire and all talking at once, brimming with enthusiasm and eager for food. Conversations would flow like springs, interlaced and sparkling like the circle of faces. The Buddha fell completely now into recollections of the roadtrip, linear time all nonsense – what is, was and is again – as the sights and sounds of friendship and delight rang around him once more...

CHAPTER II

Roadtrip

'Wake up and come out to the car.
There's an east swell coming and it's howling off shore
And we'll be lying like lions out in the sands.
But I'll be dead before you put a gun in my brother's hand.'

"Don't forget to breathe, Dodo," instructed the Buddha, pursing his lips so as not to burst into a convulsion of laughter in view of the latest contortion Dodo had managed. He would do himself an injury if he didn't relax and take a breath, but you had to admire his perseverance.

Tadasana, the mountain pose; Vrksasana, the tree pose; Virabhadrasana, warrior pose; Garudasana, eagle pose; Utkatasana, fierce pose; Parvatasana, mountain pose; Virasana, hero pose; Gomukhasana, head-of-cow pose; Adho Mukha Svanasana, dog pose and the Buddha's favourite, Ardha Chandrasna, the half-moon pose. He always had great craic with that. Could stand there for hours, suspended on one leg, ready for take-off into the universe of his imagination.

After winding down and relaxing in the Sarvangasana, Halasana, Setu Bandha, Viparita Karani and appropriately enough, Savasana, the corpse pose, Dodo would assume the Sukhasana, easy pose, while Buddha moved into the Siddhasana, perfect pose.

"Yoga for surfers," scoffed the Buddha, seemingly at random, "whatever will they think of next?"

Dodo, however, knew the Buddha was only bouncing a ball. Thanks to his early morning yoga session, he wasn't going to be drawn. There would be no slam-dunks for the Buddha this morning, just eggs easy over. An oeuf is an oeuf, thought Dodo with a smile.

The soft caress and calm of early morning is hard to beat, so the pair sat silently around the fire, soaking it in, waiting for the billy to boil. On long sally rods they would twirl and toast the bread over open flames. They both scoffed down a banana – they're very good for you, Dodo added mentally, mimicking the Buddha. As the water boiled, the morning was finally awoken proper to the aroma of a long black coffee.

Dodo spotted a pause in the rhythm of the morning talk and went for it: "Buddha," he said tentatively, "remember you promised to tell me about the birds and the bees? You said that it was maybe the most important thing I would ever learn, after surfing. What about now? Is now a good time to tell me?"

Buddha put on his most serious face, before deliberately and with some deliberation taking another sip of coffee. "This coffee is excellent, Dodo," he stalled, before stroking the stubble on his chin, acting as if he could somehow see his reflection and was pulling those faces that you do before you start to shave. With mouth distorted left, then right, now downturned, his lips forming a perfect 'O', he looked like Lon Chaney in 'Hunchback of Notre Dame'.

Suddenly, cutting through the complex silence that was settling over Buddha and Dodo, a cry of "Surf's up!" pierced the morning air. Right on cue, the expected crew began arriving for the well-worn ritual before their planned road trip, which the duo had been eagerly awaiting since the day before.

"Our little chat will have to wait for another time," the Buddha reassured Dodo with a gentle double pat on the shoulder, as he ushered him to ready more eggs and toast. "The bells, the bells," Buddha smiled to himself, "saved by the bells."

As the new arrivals settled, the banter went back and forth across the fire until everyone had been foddered. Absent friends were missed, but there would always be next time. Assembled were the Buddha, Dodo and Didge from Down Under, who had brought along his mate Wagga Wagga. Didge was a genius of an artist and possessed the most stunning drawings of insects, spiders, moths, snakes and birds, as well as all sorts of bugs, most of which the others had never seen or heard of. His paintings were so detailed that creepy crawlies looked even more spectacular, beautiful and real in still life than they did in real life.

Elsewhere around the flames, Kiwi, Biker and Guru were strangers to no one, while even Seymour and Shagmire showed up. The standing joke was that Seymour would get up at the crack of dawn, whereas Shagmire would get up on the crack of dawn. Seymour was a great swimmer. He once swam three miles off the coast of Sligo to see if someone who had gotten sucked out in a rip needed to be rescued, before swimming back and heading for a run. Seymour was like a fish in the water. He was, however, also like a fish out of water most of the time.

Also present were Dodo's friend Galapagos, Flip Flip (who had two left feet), Snag (so called as he was a sensitive, new age guy, and was always trying to solve other people's problems). There was Lava, who was – no prizes for guessing – inclined to erupt over nothing, but who was more usually referred to as Mr Lava Lava, as he constantly repeated himself in every sense of the word.

Although no one had really expected him to arrive, Nowhere Man showed up out of nowhere for the trip. As he was related to The Bunch of Violets – a singing sensation – it was generally believed that Nowhere Man got his name because he was always singing 'Nowhere Man', but that was not the case. He was actually called Nowhere Man because any time he was asked where he had been, he would simply say, "Nowhere, man". Any time he was asked where he was going, even if he had a surfboard under his oxter, he would say, "Where do you think I'm going – nowhere, man".

Sadhu, a friend of Guru's who always seemed to be smiling, also joined up for the roadtrip. No one knew much about him. There was a further lock of boys about, some of them hardcore, others strangers, first-timers, lads like Bimmy and Bosco, Johnny and a buddy of his, Zulu. Paddo San, who was just back from Japan, figured among the crowd, sporting a tan and a serious-looking Koa ukulele. He was going to break hearts with that baby.

A chap called Mixo, complete with a contagious laugh, said that his girlfriend could whistle 'The Lonesome Boatman' through a gap in her teeth. The Gunner Earley, so called 'cos he followed Arsenal, along with a happy-go-lucky lad who went as Groan, who couldn't understand, he said, why he never had a girlfriend, swelled the ranks, the latter being promised that Phil would help 'sort him out'. Much to Dodo's discomfort, there was a lock of additional boys, including Horse, Skull, Badger and Asal, who had it in for Elvis Costello, claiming he was a fraud trying to rip off the real Elvis.

There was Buzzer, Big Jack, Bear, Bowser Welch and Turkey, as well as three boys from the big smoke – namely Liam Og, Babog and Turtog, who was constantly sucking his thumb. They generally kept to themselves and spent most of their time shooting pool.

Your man Liam Og, whose father went as Willie, had fallen in for a huckster's shop which sold comics, but he blathered that the biggest earner for his greasy till was a plastic parrot on a perch outside that spewed out lucky bags containing bulls'-eyes, balloons, sherbet's fizz, gob stoppers or jar alleys every time you dropped in a tanner, while the bird squawked, "I want your money!" The kids loved it, according to Liam Og, who mortified his cousin John Paul every time he told that story. John Paul was a papal pregnancy, christened to commemorate the Pope's visit to the racecourse in Galway, where he concelebrated a youth mass with Bishop Eamonn Casey and Father Michael Cleary. John Paul himself was a sound man but was haunted by a story his mother told him of seeing a photographer from Birr who had his kidney ruptured as he stood on a milk crate trying to get a snap, after receiving the skelp of an umbrella from a woman who couldn't see the Pope giving out Holy Communion.

"You can't count on and you can't account for everyone. Even Jesus himself found it hard to pick twelve good ones," the Buddha tried to reassure Dodo, as he assessed the boisterous crew. "Just make sure you can stand over your own conduct in and out of the water."

Then there was Dorka. Dorka was the only woman on this trip. She was a real tomboy. Never out of a jeans and t-shirt, with fine short mousy hair, the smallest little nose and freckles. She was lovely, always looked you in the eye and called you by your name when she spoke to you. All the guys loved Dorka. Unfortunately, they also all fancied her and, worse again, thought that she fancied each and every one of them. Lucky for everyone, Dorka knew where to draw the line and understood that, with fellas, a lot of their lovin' goes on in their heads.

No surfari would be complete without the animals. Hippy Bill's small stray, Lanky, had run away from home again and taken up with the boxer Cerber. Cerber hadn't a clue but, with his white socks, was a real pet. The third dog tagging along was Aslan, called after you-know-who, a dozy but adorable Golden Retriever. Aslan was a useless guard dog, preferring to sleep like a baby in a foetal position. The only time he barked was in his sleep, clearly troubled by his dog dreaming. Dorka suggested that Snag should have a word with him. The menagerie was completed by Tup Tusch the turtle; a homeless Huntsman spider who went as 'Lovely', and the kookaburra, Scobie, who was the best guard dog of them all, even if Lovely was the scariest. While it was rarely – if ever – mentioned, there were suspicions that Scobie was really a cross between a parrot and a woodpecker, who had the ability, without any prompting or warning, to say, "What's the story, Scobie?" in a broad, Jackeen brogue, but not another word aside from those.

It was time to make tracks. Down the years, the Buddha had learned the art of travelling light. Too many possessions can make you possessive. He once had a high nelly that he had left at a stone-walled bridge near Ballyhuppahaun, and which had disappeared when he returned from picking hazelnuts. The Buddha had immediately assumed that he mustn't have needed it any longer and should walk some more.

The caravan, in the meantime, had been loaded in preparation for the trip. Pots and pans, wok and the other kitchen utensils; instruments galore, the djembe and didgeridoo snugly asleep in their knitted sock and sack and the boards lovingly loaded out top. The Buddha, however, went nowhere without his Jarrah rainstick and walking pole, which he had collected while on walkabout in Boranup. The painstakingly carved rainstick ensured that the soothing sound of the foreshore was never far away, and, while the walking pole served no particular purpose for the Buddha, he attested that it was the best-balanced object in the universe and always reminded him to stand upright. When Dodo pressed him as to what he would do if it disappeared like his high nelly, the Buddha admitted that he might miss it, before adding sagely that, "If it walks, it walks; it is, after all, a walking stick."

"Get down off that didge; you haven't a licence to drive it," roared Snag at Gráinne, who was located across the camp, to guffaws and galah as the convoy pulled out. Dismayed that she had been spotted spitting and struggling to perfect her mouth action on the didgeridoo, she did the only thing she could: she silenced Snag and his fellow sneers with a single digit response that would have made Harvey Smith proud, in the process living up to her name as 'she who inspires terror'.

The group sailed down through the Swan, 'Comer, Muckalee and Mullinavat on lively tunes and lively chat. "No politics or religion," ordained Shagmire, "them's the rules." He was always routinely ignored.

The first destination was 'An Trá Mór', the 'great strand', where they had first learned to surf. It would always have a special place in their hearts. Bernie, Billy and Sceach, as well as Liam, leis an madra, would be there with a warm welcome as always - even if the Iron Man was frozen stiff.

Round the Copper Coast they journeyed, only to be greeted by the glorious sight of the first rainbow of the trip. "No rain, no rainbows," consoled Snag, as they all appraised the stunning sight, deeply etched across the vista of the grey canvas skyline.

Onwards into West Cork, Clon and Skibb to check out the swell at Inchadoney, Castle Freak and Barleycove. A hundred more miles and you travel to Inch, throwing up beautiful Kerry rollers in the Kingdom, off strand and right hand reef tucked in under the Dingle Peninsula. Over the head and miles to go before we sleep, to windswept Mahereese to link up with Val. He would light the way down the bohereen with lanterns to lead us home.

Guru had put in a raid on his garden before setting off and had harvested some baby veg. Baby spuds and baby carrots, baby courgettes and sweet corn, green beans, and onions.

Versatile baby vegetables sounded a little cannibalistic and, sure enough, the pot wasn't long on before everyone started taking chunks out of and eating into each other.

"Who is the greatest hurler of all time?" That started it. "I said who is the greatest hurler of all time?" That was Lava. A blur of responses whipped up frenzied discussion:

"Impossible to tell."

"Apples and oranges."

"No comparison with the modern game."

"They were drinking back pints then; they're doing yoga now."

"It's speeded up for effect on the telly."

"'Fastest game in the world' me arse; sure no one plays it outside Ireland and even here hardly anyone plays it outside Munster."

"That's savage bad form to say that and you a Leinster man. Sure Cody's Kilkenny are the greatest team of all time."

"Yeah, thanks to a Laois man, Mick Dempsey."

"That's a dirty one! What have you got against Cody?"

"Nothin'. Never met the man; in fact I even like him. Did you see the way he put that Jack-in-the-Box Marty Morrissey back in his place? Did everything bar give him a kick in the arse and a slap of his cap."

"Put that in your Munster pipe and smoke it, Smarty."

"So, it's still only Munster and Kilkenny then."

"That's outrageous, that's sacrilegious."

"You can't leave out Offaly and Galway, no way."

"So what? It's still the greatest game in the world."

"Why don't they do the Yanks on it and call it the World Series then."

Before long, everyone seemed to be talking at once. "Lads, this is all very fine, until someone loses an eye," interjected Snag, quoting his favourite philosopher Pat Shortt and trying to restore calm.

"I'll ask again, for the first time, who's the greatest hurler of all time?" Lava Lava pulled on the ground to keep it going.

"Lads, lads, lads, as Pat Shortt himself would say: politics and religion – them's the rules, leave it out," Shagmire thundered, attempting to lay down the law.

"Hurling is sport, sure," Flip Flip ventured. Buddha, amid the bustle, shook his head in despair. This would end in tears.

"There is nothing under the sun that is not political," Sadhu claimed, just managing to be heard above the din.

"Hurling is sport; you can't bend the rules," Kiwi postulated, urging a bit of common sense.

"Wrong, wrong, wrong! Hurling is a religion, widely practised and attended to every Sunday. More people go to hurling matches now than to mass. Hurling people are passionate, devoted to their cause," argued Seymour, just out of the water after a swim.

"Fanatics, you mean. Like Muslims," Biker butted in.

"Jesus, lads, that's it. We said no religion. This is getting out of hand," Shagmire implored.

"Biker's right – they're like suicide bombers in Camross, Castletown, Clonad and Cushendall. They'd take the head off ya."

"But they'd shake hands with you then after the match," Kiwi observed dryly.

Wagga Wagga looked on disconcertedly and, wisely, stayed out of it. Nevertheless, the heart was put crossways in him when Scobie landed on his shoulder and squawked out, "What's the story, Scobie?" to howls of laughter. Peace broke out for a minute.

"Maybe you should offer it up to TV3 as a new reality show with Cody, Marty Morrissey, Ger Canning and Ger Loughnane on the panel, like The Apprentice," suggested the Buddha, hoping that the sheer stupidity of his suggestion would bring it all to an end.

"That's a massive idea, Buddha – you're a bloody genius," Lava exclaimed, latching on to the loose ball. "Cody could be the new Bill Cullen."

"And Marty Morrissey could be the new Jackie Lavin. It would be huge," Biker chipped in.

"Sounds good, but you'd need Jackie Healy-Rae in there for the common man, the non-hurling crowd – you don't want to turn them off. Sort of like the way they have Louis Walsh on X-Factor and he knows feck all about music," chimed Nowhere Man, who was just back from a walk down the beach with Dorka and who dutifully shocked everyone with his language.

"There's no need for the cursin' but Nowhere Man is right. You'd need Jackie Healy-Rae on board. That would suit TV3 for the synergy because then Jackie Lavin could be the new Jackie Healy-Rae in reverse, if you know what I mean," Flip Flip said, arriving out of nowhere himself. Buddha wondered if he had perhaps cut straight to the dessert, hitting the cáca milis before they had even eaten. "Anyway, that'd be really very good because Jackie Healy-Rae wears a wig as well." Flip Flip was clearly on a roll.

"No, you're thinking of Donnie Cassidy," corrected Seymour, a stickler for detail.

"He'll sue you for that, ye know," Snag counselled.

"Toupée or not to pay, that is the question," beamed Guru, still slaving over a hot stove of baby vegetables.

"Touché," acknowledged Didge.

"And, like I said, there's nothing under the sun that's not political," reminded Sadhu, "even the hair that's not on your head."

"Okay, let me make it easy on you then," announced Lava, who clearly hadn't spent half enough time in the water today and hadn't yet run out of steam. "Finn Mac Cumhaill, Cu Chulainn, Setanta – Ó hAilpín that is –, D.J., Eddie Kehir, Henry Shefflin, Pat O'Neill, Tommy Walsh…"

"Is there no one else other than Kilkenny and Na Fianna?" It kicked off again.

"What about Nicky Rackard, Tony Doran, Liam Mackay, Brian Corcoran and Jimmy Barry Murphy?"

"I don't have a black-and-white telly."

"What about the Waterford boys and the guts they've brought to the game, with the likes of Tony Browne, the Brick, Dan the Man and yer man Mullane?"

"Sure Clare churned out some good hurlers too. The Sparrow was a fair one."

"What about that Canning chap from Galway? He's a pure genius and they knockin' lumps out of him."

"That's his problem; it's a man's game."

"Nicky English, Babs Keating?"

"You're scraping the barrel now."

"Sure, he has only one more All Ireland medal than me."

"The Corrigans, Johnny Pilkington and the other fella off the telly, what's his name...he was very good...Michael Duignan."

"And he's good lookin' too and so is your man, Seán Óg – Ó hAilpín, that is": It was Dorka, throwing in her tuppence-worth, astounding everyone with her interest in hurling.

"Sure, you might as well include the greatest hurler of them all then, Mickey Sullivan so."

"Now that's vergin' on the ridiculous."

"After this year you can't possibly leave out Eoin Kelly and Corbett."

"Tommy Doyle was better than the two of them together."

"You can't leave out the Dooley Brothers."

"I thought they were a band?"

"If we're going down that road, what about Martin Cuddy and Pat Critchley, the greatest hurler ever not to win an All Ireland, and you might as well take in Sabu Whelan, one of our own and sure Brian Whelan."

"It's Whelehan."

"You're more of a Marty than an O'Muircheartaigh, I'll tell ye that much."

"What about them? What have you got against Offaly anyway? Would you shout for them if Laois were knocked out?"

"I would, yeah, if they were hurlin' Manchester United, I would!"

Appeals for one voice were lost amid the pandemonium and the Guru wasn't impressed when the big saucepan with all the baby veg was nearly knocked over in the agitation.

"Christy Ring. Christy Ring is the greatest hurler of all time," the Buddha's statement stunned the surfers into silence for a second.

"And?" asked Lava.

"And, wasn't that your question and there's your answer. Christy Ring, the undisputed greatest hurler of all time. Poetry in motion, a man who inspired poets and peasants, a man of profound wisdom. Christy Ring, without a shadow of a doubt, is the greatest hurler of all time."

"We'll have to put that one to Marty Morrissey," reckoned Kiwi, trying to get a rise from the Buddha.

"I thought he was a milkman," Flip Flip pondered aloud.

The Buddha continued: "He was a man commendably reluctant to give advice. Once, when pressed to offer some insight to the secret of success, and after a long hesitation, he spoke to the man on the radio and said, 'You keep your eye on the ball boy, even if the ref have it'."

"What's that supposed to mean?" Dodo whined. "Sleep on it," urged the Buddha.

"Any more gems there Buddha?" poked Lava, disappointment colouring his tone because the heat had been taken out of his debate.

"Yes, when you eat, eat." The Buddha held the high ground as Guru and Sadhu served up their scrumptious supper – a move that conclusively silenced the hungry mob.

"That was just delicious; how did you manage that again?" Dorka asked, getting on to Guru to disclose his method, which he generously divulged.

"Anyone not interested in cooking can head off or do the wash up," tendered Guru. No one left as he explained that you first bring the potatoes and carrots to the boil and, after about ten minutes, add the courgettes, sweet corn and green beans, before bringing back to the boil until they are all cooked and then straining off the water.

Next on the Buddha's wok, the cook fried off the onions until they were nice and brown and, on a lower heat, added in the chilli, garlic and ginger, making sure not to burn them. The cooked veg were put in next and tossed around in the wok. Following this, the cherry tomatoes were introduced and a good stir given, until some of the tomatoes burst. The dish was then seasoned with salt and pepper. To complete the meal and nourishment, cooked chickpeas were finally added and the food served up with some of that crusty bread that was bought off that lovely fella back in Castlegregory.

The Buddha was inspired to burst into verse:

'Looking at his corpse laid out,
 the day of his untimely death,
 a woman said: 'It would be a sin to bury such a man.'
 I have not managed yet to bury Christy Ring.
 Sometimes I imagine him
 Being venerated
 In the care of the group god, Aengus
 On a slab at Newgrange
 And at each winter solstice
 For just one half an hour
 A ray of sunshine
 Lighting up his countenance."

"Lovely hurling," complimented Dorka.

"Sweet," agreed Kiwi, to concurring nods all round. By now, everyone was just fit for the sack.

The next morning in Lahinch, the stubborn sun sat sulking in the sky, still unable to master the mysterious mist that decided it would hang around for the day. It had been the same all the way up along the west coast, as the soupy fog shrouded the shoreline at Doonbeg, Spanish Point, Cornish and Fanore. The secret spot down the lane, at the stone cottage between Lahinch and Spanish, was invisible and, up to the right-hand side of the Cliffs of Moher, Aileens was nowhere to be seen. The Aran Islands too had disappeared for the day. Dodo and Galapagos had learned a way to spectate the giant wave at the Cliffs and, after negotiating sodden fields, rusty barbed wire fences and the precarious precipice, it was a piebald bull that decided it was not wise for them to linger with the fog.

These haunts owed the group nothing, even though for hours on end, they had slept over and been stoked at Spanish Point. They'd gone doggin' it in Doonbeg, where the 19th is the Atlantic Ocean, and they'd been loving the long-boarding in Lahinch. Fanore was so much fun. Only the brave, brilliant or foolhardy would flirt with Aileens. Cornish was more to the group's speed.

"Anyone for coffee?"

Disappointed with the lack of recent surfing opportunities, the Buddha tried to be philosophical. "I suppose surfing is a bit like life itself; ninety per cent paddling and pushing out against the swell and ten per cent riding the waves."

"Sure thing," consoled Sadhu. "There's a time to surf and a time to wax your board. Today, we repair."

Buddha had hoped that today would be the day he would finally paddle out to Aileens, the monster wave at the foot of the Cliffs of Moher. Go to Galicia when you can, he had always advised, as you never knew when you might get another chance. He had longed to try to master the great wave – that and his own fear, swelling up inside him even at the thoughts of it. What a sight it would be to take Aileens and caress and slide down her leek-leaf-green and blue hair, all the way from top to bottom, before you would slip away without awakening her, like a satisfied lover in the early morning.

Then there were those puffins. Odd and awkward, seemingly billions of them, clinging to the edge of the world, making sure to do their business before they too took off one morning without saying a word. The puffins are gone. Then, of course, there was Dodo and the matter of the birds and the bees. Buddha desperately needed to surf.

"Ninety-nine per cent paddling, one per cent riding; sound familiar? Sounds like every relationship I've ever been in," the big dozy head of Wagga Wagga emerged from the two-man, which was harbouring at least three bodies.

"What would you know about love?" came the call to arms from Kiwi.

"Mountain men love mountain women," Mixo intoned, regarding himself as a bit of an expert in affairs of the heart, as he too appeared to tumble out of the two-man.

"Ye boys need a tee pee and no one is ever goin' to love you as much as you love yourself," sounded Bosco, getting off a shot across Mixo's bow, whatever the bad blood was between that pair.

"What's love got to do with it?" trumpeted Zulu, and so the battle lines were drawn, the coffee and commotion waking the dead.

"It all depends on how you look at it. Life and love, love in life, is different for everyone. There are many different types of love, all true, but not necessarily all the same," reasoned Seymour.

"Jaysus, you're starting to sound like the Buddha. I'm getting a bit worried about ye boys." Biker was up and at it.

"Like it says in that new book: 'Women are from Venus, men are from bars'."

"Well, what's the difference between a mural and graffiti? Both paintings on a wall, creative, provocative, interesting and inspiring and yet one is considered art and the other, anarchy. One artist commended and lauded, the other criticised and outlawed. Who can tell you what art is? Who can tell you that this is love?" pondered the Buddha, never one to use one sentence when a thousand would do.

"What you're really trying to say is that one man's Art is another man's Muriel," sideswiped Flip Flip, sporting one of his t-shirts (which seemingly numbered thousands). The Buddha was unable to make out from his tone if he was being sincere or sneering.

Dodo claimed that Flip Flip had 367 t-shirts, with various slogans on them that he couldn't make head nor tail of; one for every day of the year. Today's masterpiece was 'Che Who? Che Vous?', replacing one with 'The End is Night' on the front and 'Tempest Fugit' on the back. The Buddha knew he had to have a quiet word with Flip Flip.

"Love is blind," Biker pronounced, having arrived on the scene.

"Only if it's love at first site," Big Jack maintained as he ambled in. "Surely you mean first sight?" Dodo asked, passing Jack a steaming coffee mug. "No, I mean first site, but nothing less than four hundred acres of course," rebounded the big man, to appreciative smiles all round.

"What's love got to do, got to do, got to do with it? What's love but a second-hand emotion..." Nowhere Man came out of nowhere, strutting like a bantam cock as he crowed his rendition of Tina Turner, his mimic of her on stage even worse than his singing.

"A girl crying is the saddest sound in the whole world," Sadhu murmured in a serious tone. "I once heard a girl sobbing her heart out in the shadows near the harbour of Santander and swore I never wanted to be the cause of crying like that ever again."

The Buddha seized upon the silence. "There was an old woman in China who had supported a monk for over twenty years. She had built a little hut for him and fed him while he was meditating. Finally, she wondered just what progress he had made in all this time.

"To find out, she obtained the help of a girl rich in desire. 'Go and embrace him,' she told her, 'and then ask him suddenly: "What now?"'

"The girl called upon the monk and, without much ado, caressed him, asking him what he was going to do about it.

"'An old tree grows on a cold rock in winter,' replied the monk, somewhat poetically. 'Nowhere is there any warmth.'

"The girl returned and related what he had said.

"'To think I fed that fellow for twenty years!' said the old woman in anger. 'He showed no consideration for your need, no disposition to explain your condition. He need not have responded to passion but at least he should have evidenced some compassion.'"

"She at once went to the hut of the monk and burned it down."

"Sounds like my mother-in-law," quipped Zulu, who was having none of the touchy-feely stuff.

"'If I speak with the tongues of men and of angels, but do not have love, I have become a noisy gong or a clanging cymbal. If I have the gift of prophecy, and know all mysteries and all knowledge; and if I have all faith, so as to remove mountains, but do not have love, I am nothing. And if I give all my possessions to feed the poor, and if I surrender my body to be burned, but do not have love, it profits me nothing.

"'Love is patient,
love is kind and is not jealous;
love does not brag and is not arrogant,
does not act unbecomingly;
it does not seek its own,
is not provoked, does not take into account a wrong suffered,
does not rejoice in unrighteousness, but rejoices with the truth;
bears all things, believes all things, hopes all things, endures all things.
Love never fails,'" recited Guru, who was not too busy with preparing the morning vittles to enter the fray.

"Wow, what was that?" Shagmire had surfaced.

"A letter."

"Lucky girl."

"A letter from St Paul to the Corinthians."

"Jesus, now you have me. Corinthians – they're not from this parish anyway."

"It's in the Bible," Sadhu pointed out, sure that his prompt would stir some hint of recognition, but the blank faces peering out over mugs said it all.

"We're waiting for it to come out on DVD," Zulu let fly to gales of laughter, the crew nodding in agreement at his superior knowledge, as one of his many business interests was a video store that specialised in westerns and war movies.

"What's so funny?" Dorka entreated, as her delightful smile and sparkling eyes thanked Guru for the scrambled eggs with fresh chives and honey toast.

"Love, that's what's funny," muttered someone or other, as by now nearly everyone was milling about. "What about you, have you ever been in love, Dorka?" Turtog was feeling brave enough to ask, but would have to get up much earlier to flummox Dorka.

"Did you come down in the last shower or arrive on Wanderly Wagon, lover boy?" Dorka bitch-slapped him with her retort, as veterans of these trips smiled in satisfaction that she hadn't lost her touch, before smugly sitting back to await the coup de grâce.

"'Twenty monks and one nun – who was named Eshun – were practising meditation with a certain Zen master. Eshun was very pretty, even though her head was shaved and her dress plain. Several monks secretly fell in love with her. One of them wrote her a love letter, insisting upon a private meeting. Eshun did not reply. The following day, the master gave a lecture to the group, and when it was over, Eshun arose. Addressing the one who had written her, she said: 'If you really love me so much, come and embrace me now.'" Dorka hạd clearly taken a leaf out of the Buddha's book, and there were blushes and shuffling of feet all round.

"As Jerry Lee Lewis said to Chuck Berry when he set fire to the piano on stage in Memphis, 'follow that!'" Snag exclaimed, relishing the moment, as others opted to skulk away from the blaze.

"Let's head for Mayo," Sadhu suggested, making a clearing for those in retreat. Biker responded, as bubbly as ever, "Up Mayo, and Sally O'Brien and the way she might look at ye!"

Mayo – a magical place. Its haunting heather and mysterious marshes hide a million secrets. The ocean that meets it is constantly testing and pushing its luck. There are secrets and dark secrets, both as difficult to distil, but each leaving a much different taste in the mouth. The skeletons of elk, the carcasses of whales and the dreams of people are buried here, with little enough to mark the spot now, other than rust and relics. Their ghosts are hanging in the air, abandoned, awaiting a proper burial. The Buddha wanted to move on, but found it difficult to forget.

A pit stop was agreed upon, with time to check out Carrowniskey and an excuse for coffee and chat.

"We're going to have a whale of a time; you can't beat Achill Head for the craic," Babog bellowed. The Jackeen was beginning to grate on the Buddha and he cut him in two with a look.

Guru ambled by, pointedly singing, "If looks could kill they probably will". Buddha got the message and left it so.

"What about the secret spots?" enthused Bimmy, with genuine curiosity.

"They don't call them secret spots for nothing. If you don't know where they are, then you are not ready to surf them," reasoned Seymour.

"And if we told you where they were, you know we would have to..." Sadhu jested with Bimmy, who quickly cottoned on.

The day was still young when they rocked up to Keel Beach and sought out the Black fella and the artist formerly known as Shane, as them boys would know the score on camping and conditions. There was an honest groundswell rolling in under the eye of the Minnaun Cliffs and the winds were offshore. Such a perfect day, with perfect lines, perfect sets and not a second to waste in soaking it up.

"I want to spend it with you," crooned Biker, who was, maryah, slow waltzing with himself, and his wet suit only half on.

The Buddha always said that surfing was good for the head, great for the heart and mighty for the soul. On days like today, you simply couldn't beat the west coast. Mellow day and mellow out.

Dodo, meanwhile, was frantically waxing his board.

"I feel like a little boy let loose with a box of crayons," Snag observed, as he too administered a new layer of the coconut-scented wax. The Buddha nodded with pleasure and approval.

The Buddha knew that once he was in the water, nothing else matters. He had been a slow learner but had come to understand that surfing is out of this world. The water was waiting to wash away all his aches and woes. They would dissolve in the water and be washed out to sea.

"Do you hope to find enlightenment on this trip, Buddha?" taunted Turtog. The Buddha decided that this boy had a long road ahead of him and it was a long road that had no turn on it.

"I'll settle for a good wave, a good book and a tasty recipe for dukkah," the Buddha returned, letting it slide.

The Buddha looked proudly over his quiver of boards. Big Red, The Log, The Ark, Gráinneuaille – which was dubbed 'The Whale' for short – and the Queen Mary. They were all over nine feet long and virtually identical in width and girth. "They all please me in different ways," he was fond of saying, deflecting criticism of the pointlessness of a selection of boards that were all the same. "As far as I'm concerned, short boards are for chaps.

When it comes to surfing, size matters. A good surfboard is like a good woman: forgiving, and, once you find her sweet spot, happy days. Anyway, I'm looking for nourishment, not punishment," he would preach to anyone within range, but by now he was talking to himself, paddy last in the water.

Out in the line-up, the Buddha liked to linger and lap it up. The towns and villages, the lie of the land – everything looked different from here. Everything was smaller in the water, even problems.

"You missed that one, Buddha," said Babog, prompting the Buddha to fleetingly contemplate the prospects of a drowning 'accident'. A surface-skimming 'V' formation of arctic tern provided sufficient distraction and he moved on.

"They're waves, not Dublin Bus – there'll be another one along in a few seconds," scorned Seymour, realising that it was a matter of pearls and pigs before the words had left his mouth.

Without a word, only a wide-eyed and gentle nod to those in the know heralded the best set of the day, breaking left and right. Buddha and Guru, who had been sitting out the back, effortlessly pivoted towards the shore with a gentle stroke of the hand, barely caressing the surface. A duck-like motion of the legs, which had been straddling the board, followed, with thighs hugging the rails. Popping forward now, prone, sweet spot. Deep breath. Arched back. Then to shoulder-deep strokes. Paddle deep and deliberate, no scrawbing. Sweet spot, sweet motion and a quick glance back. Deeper now, at pace: the wave is coming. Don't forget to breathe, as the wave will not wait if you're not ready. It might roar by, laughing at your best, or, if mischievous enough, turn you topsy-turvy, arse over head, your whole world upside down, wiped out in a tumble dryer of delight that doesn't stop till you scrape the sand, letting you know who's still boss.

Off the shoulder as she rolled over, the Buddha was up. Steady, stay low, as simple as sitting on a high stool. Drop down the face. Grind into the groove. Lean against the edge, leash leg back over the fin. Perfect balance, up and down. This wave's got spine and stamina, stiff and strong, the breeze in its face feathering foam off the top. The sea surges, sensing the shore. Water gushing over the tail. Buddha balances, ballerina-like, along the board, hanging five. Ease back a little and enjoy the rest of the ride. Lazy boy. Sheer joy.

Last in and last out, the crew had already adjourned to the shelter of Keem Bay for the evening. The setting sun headed for the horizon but for the moment looked as if it was impossibly and precariously perched atop the arch of a rainbow. If you painted the picture, no one would believe you, especially not with those madcap fluffy clouds. The lapping surf sounded as if it too was taking a rest, with a crescent moon winking down from behind the furze-filled hill, which completed the moat on their perfect sanctuary. There was every chance they would spot a pod of dolphins or even get to swim in that cove with a basking shark – that is, those swimmers trusting enough to believe that the monster fish only surfaced to suck up plankton.

Sadhu and Guru were already slaving over a hot stove, as many hands made light work for a spiced cashew nut paella supper. Both the sound of it and the whiff of saffron only made the Buddha long for Galicia and his friends there, Xan, Ivan and Moss. Didge and Paddo San were also busy, strumming and stoking up the tunes.

"What advice would you give those shortboard boys now, Buddha?" Harmless as you like, Flip Flip queried, but anybody could see that one coming for miles.

"I'd tell them, 'Go surfing when you can.'" The Buddha was too mellow now to bother rising to the bait.

"Never eat yellow snow," says Lava Lava.

"Don't build your house in a hollow," Snag followed up.

"Never trust someone who doesn't dance," maintained Didge, disputing a chord change with Paddo San.

"Never, ever drink and jive."

"Clarity begins at home."

"Absinthe makes the heart grow fonder."

"There are plenty of fish in the sea."

An avalanche of advice tumbled down the hillside. Sometimes, Dodo thought there was so much advice that it all sounded like an orchestra of vuvuzelas inside his head. He would stick with Christy Ring and keep his eye on the ball.

"Should we be afraid of a basking shark if it shows up?" asked Gunner, half fancying a twilight dip.

"There are more dangerous sharks than the basking shark," insisted Seymour, adding, "Sharks just get a bad press".

"Well, let me put it this way to you," Buddha butted in. "Thanks to John Wayne and Johnny Weissmuller, most people are afraid of crickets, Comanches and the kookaburra, whereas they should be on the lookout for the cuckoo, pilgrim. The basking shark has never been known to bite anyone yet."

"Or take their nest, Cheetah," said Dodo.

The scent of saffron served notice of the feast being prepared on the open flames. Lanky and Aslan sniffed and paced until they found a cosy spot sandwiched between Dorka and the fire, where they were soon snoring.

Didge and Bongo on the drums kept the rhythm of the night, as Paddo San sang his heart out on requests. Strangers ebbed and flowed, as did a dozen conversations. Friendly nods, high fives, hugs and shakas of friendship swelled at the delight of familiar faces. There was a great buzz about when two more fellas squatted down.

"As I haven't yet mastered the knack of the loaves and the fishes, you may give me that third big pot over," Sadhu requisitioned, as surfers took turns in the line-up to chop onions, garlic, chilli, carrots, cashew nuts, tomatoes, courgette and peppers, which would be seasoned up with the saffron, salt, paprika, pepper and lemon. A stubble-pussed Seymour looked dangerously like Jack Nicholson, framed in the dancing flames as he vigorously chopped fresh coriander to dress the dish, holding a ridiculously long knife and unwittingly keeping beat with the bongos. In a fourth saucepan, Guru was stirring in short-grain brown rice.

"Great for the nerves, lots of vitamins and minerals," he maintained, with that broad, smiling cookin' head on him. The food and the evening were bubbling and coming along nicely.

As Didge, Paddo San and Bongo consulted the chords on the next tune, Banjo threw a spanner in the spokes and called for a Wolfe Tones ballad. It was fortunate that he didn't know the words of it himself and it was the luck of God altogether that he hadn't brought his banjo with him, for fear of getting drunk and forgetting it. Otherwise, he'd have had a stab at it anyway.

"Sit down there Banjo and chop some garlic," ordered Guru, distracting him in the process and, as he hadn't his mind a minute, he forgot all about the Wolfe Tones.

The stranger with the pale face and a chin that could chop cabbage in a milk bottle took into a poem:

"We're almost home, pet, almost home...
 Our home is at...
 I'll be home...
 I have to go home now...
 I want to go home now...
 Are you feeling homesick?
 Are you anxious to get home? ...
 I can't wait to get home...
 Let's stay at home tonight and...
 What time will you be coming home at? ...
 If I'm not home by six at the latest, I'll phone...
 We're nearly home, don't worry, we're nearly home...
 Homeless in Dublin,
 Blown about the suburban streets at evening,
 Peering in the windows of other people's homes,
 Wondering what it must feel like
 To be sitting around a fire –
 Apache or Cherokee or Bourgeoisie –
 Beholding the firelit faces of your family,
 Beholding their starry or their TV gaze:
 Windfall to Windfall – can you hear me?
 Windfall to Windfall...

We're almost home, pet, don't worry anymore, we're almost home."

Dorka discreetly passed a tissue to Shagmire as his eyes glazed over. The stranger smiled, beaming, and said he fancied a walk on the strand "before din-dins". He then took off with his friend, heading down the slope for the strand.

"What was that?"

"Who was that?"

Phil said that the stranger's friend had told him his life was a bit helter skelter and that he was heading to Cali to sort out his head. Phil, who was from that neck of the woods, said to check him out if he ever got to Mission Beach, where they'd go surfing with the pelicans.

"He said his name was Charlie, that he was on a mission, but one that didn't include San Diego," Phil recalled, before taking up the ukulele and strumming a familiar intro, trying to get the evening back on track.

"That boy needs to chill big time," observed Snag.

"Poor Charlie don't surf," sympathised Dorka.

"And the homeless paleface one isn't helping his stress levels either," noted Banjo, who was now mowing through enough garlic to feed an army, but at least it kept him out of harm's way.

"Your education is sadly neglected; that friend is Durcan and he's from these parts," the Buddha intervened, still eyeing the pair who were making their winding way towards the beach.

"'Goodbye Mursheen Durkin, I'm sick and tired of workin', no more I'll dig the praties, no longer I'll be poor; for as sure as me name is Carney I'll be off to California, where instead of diggin' praties, I'll be diggin' lumps of gold.' That Durkin?" lilted Biker.

"No, Paul Durcan, no relation. Paul Durcan, Ireland's greatest living poet," the Buddha said.

"A fierce man for the sad verse," poked Paddo San, everyone else thinking him hilarious, except the Buddha.

"Greatest living poet me arse, sure what about Heaney? Heaney's the man and all the stuff he wrote on the Troubles. Your man's not in that league, where 'hope and history' rhyme," Liam Og weighed in.

"This is all very fine until someone loses an eye," remarked Seymour, who was still brandishing that big blade.

"Heaney's poems never rhymed for me; he never wrote about my troubles. Heaney sold out. Heaney's overrated. Durcan is Ireland's greatest living poet because he's lived and he's alive to tell the tale." Thus, the Buddha laid down the law and when he was in this humour, he wasn't worth besting.

"If my boy says he can eat fifty eggs, he can eat fifty eggs," announced Paddo San, who was still up to his devilment, in a southern drawl that would do Dragline proud.

"Good night John-Boy."

"Good night Mary Ellen."

"Good night, Lucille." The giggles were doing the rounds and even the Buddha had to burst into laughter as the grub was dished out – and not before time.

"Who's the world's greatest surfer so, seeing as we have the hurling and poetry sorted," asked Kiwi, who couldn't help himself.

"Has to be the Duke, Duke Kahanamoku," insisted Seymour, more by way of getting the ball rolling.

"Jesus, I thought you meant John Wayne for a minute," gasped Guru. Contenders' names were in no short supply.

"Has to be Taj."

"No, Mick Fanning."

"Rob Machado is the man."

"Laird Hamilton."

"What about Fergal Smith? He's right up there."

"Here we go again, parochial."

"John McCarthy – did ye see him in the bank advert?"

"Bank ad?! That's too much; who started this?"

"I can't bear it, stop now."

"What about the women?"

"Stop it now before someone gets hurt."

"Bank ad – that's totally fecked up."

"There's no need for that at all."

"Woody Brown, John Severson, Gerry Lopez, Luis Gustavo Lima, Richard Brewer, Nat Young, Pedro Bastos Cunha, Tom Curren, Titus Kinimaka, George Freeth, Vincent Biagiotti..." The names kept rolling in, one for every wave.

"Joel Parkinson, Mark Occhilupo, Dickie Fitz, Mickey Sullivan, The Wolfe Tones..."

"Someone help," begged Seymour.

"Kelly, it has to be Kelly — the best surfer in the world." The Buddha's suggestion was spoken with finality, in a bid to restore some order, and was met with general nods of agreement.

"Kelly Slater, nine-time world champion, the best surfer of his generation and all time," Flip Flip summed up.

"No, Peter Kelly, from Shanahoe," pounced the Buddha, to much surprise. "The best surfer in the world is the surfer who enjoys surfing the most, and that's Peter Kelly, without a shadow of a doubt. He's the best surfer in the world, in and out of the water," Buddha said, amid sounds of approval.

Phil hit the opening Crazy Horse chords on the guitar with intent. Paddo San was tight behind on the ukulele, as Bongo and Didge revved up the rhythm section.

"Long ago in the book of old,
  Before the chapter
  where dreams unfold.
  A battle raged
  on the open page,
  Love was a winner there
  overcoming hate
  Like a little girl
  who couldn't wait."

Needing no invitation, everyone promptly joined in, singing, dancing, grooving and moving. Stargazing until they ran out of songs. Perfect sets, songs and waves all night. Such delight.

"Love and only love
  will endure
  Hate is everything
  you think it is
  Love and only love
  will break it down
  Love and only love,
  will break it down
  Break it down, break it down."

The next morning, it wasn't the mist that dampened spirits but rather the mush of a sea. It didn't seem possible that it was the same place. Overnight, the wind had sneaked round and come full onshore. The hardcore among the group got in for a dip but to no avail. It was like trying to surf in a milk churn.

"Water coming at you from all angles, more backwash goin' out than swell coming in and the wind blowing a gale in your snot on the paddle out. It's like trying to ride a bad ass in the Grand National," said a crestfallen Biker, summing up the conditions for anyone still in doubt. It was time to bid Achill adieu.

It was off to Enniscrone, Easkey, Strandhill and Streedagh, with a few more secret spots waiting in Sligo, before they would break for Bundoran's peak, Tullan and Rossnowlagh. The Causeway coast and the promise of Portrush could not be passed, before setting sail for Cotes de Basques, Hendaye, Pantin, Frouxeira, Campelo and the Costa da Morte, afterwards plunging south for Sagres, Cordoama and Praia de Vale Figueiros, with its gorgeous goose barnacles and the hidden gem of Ponta Ruiva – quite an experience in the safe hands of the Toby tribe.

First, however, the Buddha would make a detour for Dooey, across the Gweebarra and down through Lettermacaward, making up for lost time with Hippy Bill, bringing Lanky home and, hopefully, KT would be about for some tips on surfing and fishing. He was as sound as a trout and with more luck, his brother – the Legend – would be home from California in time to test the water for the Inter-Counties in Rossnowlagh. They didn't call him 'the Legend' for nothing.

In Dooey, you could avoid the din. In Dooey, you could get lost. They would stuff themselves on short stories, tall tales and conspiracy theories, after selfishly surfing to their satisfaction. With crusty bread, they would mop porridge-fattened mussels and soak up more than their fill of stories, until their souls and senses surfed with delight into the night.

The freshest of mussels, steaming in just enough water to prise them open, with a hint of red wine, chopped chillies and garlic to tackle the briny tang. A hearty supper – rocket fuel for rainbow warriors, hippies all, hell-bent on subversion. A second plantation. A dawn surf at Dooey and the world is your oyster.

"That Charlie fella was as odd as two socks, and as for your poet Durcan, he sure went on and on about his father and mother, the Russians and Volkswagens," Dodo declared. He was still trying to distil the last few nights' happenings, to see if he had been dreaming. The Buddha, by contrast, had moved on. He was surfing. The waves in Dooey were deadly, deadly fun.

"It's not the mothers and fathers I blame at all; it's the parents," Dodo continued. As the Buddha suspected, Dodo kept blabbing away, regurgitating something else he had half heard over the old flames in Achill, something about poetry readings in the Bridge House and Kelly's Hotel in Tullamore and Portlaoise.

Without a whisper, the Buddha was gone. Only the back of his head remained visible, now that he had shot down the front of the wave, dropping his shoulder, swivelling his hips slightly to gain advantage, then leaning forward for the speed as he shot along the inside of the wall, fingering the water gently to steer through the spray. Heaven.

Dodo, though, was a different story. He had nosedived and wiped out. Truly, the waves in Dooey barrelled up out of the blue. The surfacing sun had been momentarily eclipsed as this baby welled up to erase the horizon. Dodo was still yapping about the poetry reading in Portlaoise when the wave took him and, like a rag doll, dismissed him into the deep. He plunged head-first, his chin catching the lip of the board as he lunged forward, out of control, lucky not to greet the board again as it speared back into the water when he resurfaced, with a bruised ego and sore chin, coughing and spluttering, spewing salty sea out of his nostrils like a marine iguana. Disgusted.

With nothing wounded worse than his pride, Dodo had learned his lesson.

"As Christy Ring might say..." Buddha began, consoling him as they both paddled back out to finish on a good wave. Dodo good-humouredly acknowledged in an exaggerated Cork accent: "You keep your eye on the ball boy, even if the ref have it."

"Sure, everyday's a school day," reflected the Buddha.

It was coming up to nine by the time the pair made for the bohereen back up to Bill's for breakfast. Down along the dunes however, they stood agape at the strangest sight ever. Further up the sand, casting long shadows as they came out of the sun, were nineteen men, all dressed in suits.

"Where in the name of God are these boys goin' in that get-up?" Dodo was entitled to wonder aloud, even with water still running out of his nose. "Probably tell you, to see a man about a dog," guessed the Buddha, who was, in all his days, equally confounded.

As the group came towards them, they were smiling and civil, even stopping to exchange greetings and good tidings for the day – they in their pin stripes, the pair in their wet suits.

The nineteen, each of whom looked like they weren't much more than nineteen, all wore name tags – Khalid Almihdhar, Majed Moqed, Nawaf Alhazmi, Salem Alhazmi, Hani Hanjour, Satam Al Suqami, Waleed Alshehri, Wail Alshehri, Mohamed Atta, Abdulaziz Alomari, Marwan Al-Shehhi, Fayez Rashid Ahmed Hassan Al Qadi Banihammad, Ahmed Alghamdi, Hamza Alghamdi, Mohand Alshehri, Saeed Alghamdi, Ahmed Ibrahim Al Haznawi, Ahmed Alnami and Ziad Samir Jarrah.

They headed up the hill and disappeared into thin air as Buddha and Dodo came over the brow, lucky not to be bowled over by a bald-headed farmer in a bald-tyred tractor, its rusty frame as rugged as his own, with matching sideburns and a gap in his front teeth resembling where the Massey's safety cabin used to be. It was Bill.

"It takes all sorts, I suppose," Dodo later pondered as he sat into a platter of free-range eggs and brown bread in Bill's house.

"You'll certainly come across all sorts in Donegal," the Buddha opined with a shrug.

"Back in Ballyhuppahaun too, I bet," Bill added.

"Well, as you say Buddha, 'every day's a school day,' but it seemed to me they were from somewhere sunnier than Donegal altogether," said Dodo, who had the last word as he topped another googie.

In the warm glow of the day, Buddha's mind wandered again, back to Świętokrzyski and its wonderful witches. He wondered idly what mischief they'd be getting up to now, with their Sabbaths and their celebrations.

CHAPTER III

Surfing in Świętokrzyski

*'Do ritheamar trasna trí ruilleogach
Is do ghluais an comhrac ar fud na muinge,
Is treascairt dá bhfuair sé sna turtóga
Chuas ina ainneoin ar a dhroim le fuinneamh.
Alliliú puilliliu, alliliú tá an poc ar buile.'*

Raven-haired Ruth and Rebecca roared hysterically as they hurtled down the hill by the side of Łysa Góra. The pair were as mad as March hares. Just for devilment, they had hitched a piggyback ride on a long-horned, Bald Mountain puck goat who had got the better of them as they rode, cowgirl style, and clung on for dear life to his shaggy grey beard.

Riding bareback, they bawled as the billy goat belted breakneck for the Black Pool, cowbells clanking around its neck, chiming in the cacophony and consternation, while anyone and anything in the way were sent flying by *lejak*.

Tsutomu Yamaguchi was the last one to be bundled over, his basket of herbs scattered to the four winds, before the two reckless witches ended up dumped in the water. The unwitting goat, glad to be shut of them, tucked into his windfall bouquet garni.

"That's what I call a proper rampage," asserted Ruth, vowing that she would yet tame the Yellowstone rogue goat.

The brunette Grażyna, blonde Gráinne and flame-headed Grace and Gee looked on, barely batting an eyelid at these high jinks. After all, they had the Witches' Sabbath to attend and their legendary concoctions and music wouldn't magically blend themselves. Inspiration was fine for poets but perspiration and precision worked best when it came to throwing the most infamous parties in Europe.

With the Harvest Moon Gatherings now over, the hordes would doubtless descend upon the Świętokrzyski Mountains for Samhain. Its sprawling and bountiful plains were home to many a bohemian. Others would flock to their autumn hideout on their way back from walkabout. Hippies and hangers-on, druids and dodgers, sea shepherds, surfers, Rainbow Travellers and their cohorts could all be expected.

There was space here and lots of grass, slopes on which to roll and loll. There were forests of fir, oak and beech, to which the birds flocked. Finches, tits and warblers nested and rested there, bending branches to their best. Long-tailed tit, bearded tit, marsh tit, willow tit, crested tit, coal tit, blue tit and great tit, green finch and gold finch, garden warbler, Bonelli's warbler, willow warbler, chiffchaff and hooting great owls too.

The three lakes shimmered there too: the healing waters of the Black Pool, the unvoyaged depths of the Great Pond and the super surfing sets of the Sea Eye. Room to roam and ramble towards the sheltering ridges and peaks above, the comfort and camaraderie beneath the quartzite boulder walls. Friends and wandering folk were welcome here in the bosom of Świętokrzyski, to wander amid its madness, mysteries and goats.

Surfing at Samhain in Świętokrzyski – what joy – where the heavens and earth and sea are joined.

CHAPTER IV

The King and I

'I am not your rolling wheels
I am the Highway
I am not your carpet ride
I am the sky.'

In these parts, the Dong was all-powerful. This fact wasn't lost on the Buddha, who fully realised what was at stake. His deft skills of diplomacy would have to be finely tuned if he and his comrades were to ever tell this tale around a campfire. Travelling into the belly of Dong country put the Buddha's famed and precarious balancing act on the daunting Carrick-a-Rede rope bridge in the shade, even if it spans the million-mile gorge in the north territories.

There was a frantic, ant-like activity on every street, corner and corridor throughout this kingdom, with its domes and palaces. The commotion for Buddha and his crew's welcome was, he felt, over the top, as they wound their way towards The Room.

King Dong ruled over all he could survey from the towering turrets that rocketed out of the sand. He held sway in parts that could not be seen from the highest lookout, and further still to places he would never see, not even if he was to embark now and not turn back until the end of his days.

The tribes, clans and races had sworn allegiance to this mighty monarch, adjudging it better and more bountiful for all to caress him rather than to cross him. King Dong was the seventh son of the seventh Emir in line to the throne, and was religiously voted into power every seven years by his adoring followers. He was a second cousin, once removed on his mother's side, to the Sultans of Ping and the Omars of Sharif. With connections and support like this, he was the most powerful ruler anyone could recall since records began. His strength and his success in all matters were unassailable and unrivalled.

Right now, the Buddha would have preferred to be anywhere than here in the Dongdom. After the gathering of the Harvest Moons, he had planned to go gallivanting and eventually head for the wonderful witches and their

Samhain shenanigans at Świętokrzyski. But no, thanks to Ban Ki-Moon and the Dilly Dalai he was stuck here with his motley crew (not metaphorically but quite literally) between a rock and a hard place. He idly considered ways that he might thank that couple for dispatching him and Dodo as envoys, should that opportunity ever now arise.

Buddha and Dodo were accompanied for safe passage and a show of respect by Kilkenny the Kentrosaurus; Drimoleague the Dilong and Youghal the Yangchuanosaurus. All three had big hearts that were in the right place. They had no go-back in them and had volunteered to accompany the Buddha and Dodo to the Dongdom. However, the Buddha feared their reverence would not be reciprocated in these parts and he counselled them accordingly. "Discretion will be the better part of valour," he had whispered to Drimoleague as they journeyed across the Windy Gap, before ascending into the Dongdom and the dangers that lurked therein.

"Respect, Buddha," hailed the King.

"Massive respect, Mighty Dong," replied the Buddha with a shaka, not at all surprised that the Dong's druids had done their homework and advised on his customary greeting. He himself had learned that a short upward nod sometimes passed for courtesy hereabouts. Without even offering refreshments, the King cut to the chase.

"Our people need your help. We are running out of space and losing sight of the sun, so we must build more and upwards. This must be done sooner rather than later. Time is of the essence, time is money and we have no time to waste."

That was a mouthful for the Buddha to digest. Time is money – what ridiculous raiméis, he thought. But the Buddha would bite his tongue and live, if not to fight, at least to love, another day.

"I am acting on the best available advice," continued the King, undaunted by the Buddha's silence, taking it only as confirmation of agreement. "We must build. We must build the biggest and the best building in the world, ever," brayed the Dong, his voice echoing down the cavernous corridors.

Inside, the Buddha was smiling, although not at anything the Dong was saying, as he had stopped listening from the get-go. The echoing pronouncement simply reminded him of the time when, as children, he and Dodo would cast their voices across the great canyon for the joy of hearing their return. How much fun they had back then, listening to the sounds of their own voices. The King had clearly not grown out of it.

The Dong was surrounded by his Cabinette and most influential Senators, but also (and as always) by his bodyguards – the fiercest and closest to him being the hawk-eyed Zako, his brother by another mother. There were others too: Nobs, big shots from Nob Nation, which was a principality to the sunny south and a protectorate of the Dong. It was the finance from these big Nobs that bankrolled the kingdom – and most especially now that the Dong's latest escapade, which he called The Twin Towers of Power. He smugly revealed the nom de delight he had conjured for the magnificent edifice to adoring dignitaries, whose gentile applause burst into spontaneous, rapturous cheering and hooting and full-blooded bualadh bos, as the Dong panned the room to audit the reaction.

"My advisors were stunned. After they had been working on it for months on end, I simply walked into the theatre and, after one glance – a moment of enlightenment – said the four simple words, 'The Twin Towers of Power', summing everything up. I am not very surprised that the Nobs and Senators embraced it so enthusiastically, only it seemed to take a few seconds for some of the slower ones to get it."

The King was on a charge. As the vino flowed, so too did the verbiage and voltage in the room. So much for 'in vino veritas', thought the Buddha. You have to listen to thunder, but this lot trumped any of the bull he had ever heard. The flowing wine did not engage the Dong however, and he was working The Room, scarcely, if ever, sipping from his goblet.

"Come with me, Buddha," the Dong summarily commanded, circling around and cutting off Dodo and the rest of their crew. Nodding in the direction of Buddha's cohorts, Dong added: "They will be fine, and since you and I have so much in common and so much to discuss, let's get away from the din."

"Where are your Sherpas, Buddha? Where are your caravan and your things? We will have to settle you in comfortably, make you feel at home.

Embedded is best and safest."

"What you see is what you get. You can take us as you find us, kindly King," the Buddha explained.

Unconvinced, the Dong responded: "Come now Buddha, no need for rhyme and riddles. Say what you must – you know the Dong is the one you can trust."

"No disrespect Dong, but I say what I can, as I am, admittedly, only one man. Therefore, I must say what I mean and mean what I say: all we own is right here mighty Dong, not one morsel more to fill one line in this song."

The Dong was tiring of this tilt as he watched the Buddha, replete in his ragged sarong, satchel over one shoulder and wok on the other.

"We truly travel light, as we have no might, but where, if necessary, can take flight in the night," the Buddha lilted, not wishing to rile the royal one.

"Of course; a man of mystery, words and wit, Buddha, pardon my intrigue," the Dong jeered, mentally scolding himself for almost letting his mask slip. For now, he needed the Buddha and this one was more agile than his frame suggested. No, this lump would not be larding the lean earth as he walked, but slipping silently back into the dark, as slithery as a fish in a black mountain pool, never to be stuck again.

"Is it true, Buddha, that you have won the wisdom of the wizards, the knowledge of the ages? So they say."

"Is that what they say?" asked the Buddha in feigned surprise.

"Yes, and it would profit us all if you looked after your words, especially the ones where you say what you mean and mean what you say." The Dong's voice dripped with menace as he added, "Then Zako here would not have to be mean, and it would mean that no one would have to eat their words... for starters."

They had moved from draughts to chess, it seemed, and this was a check from the Dong. The Buddha often preached that discretion is the better part of valour. He had not realised until now that Zako, the Dong's loyal lapdog, was lurking in the shadows and, as the Buddha often admitted to being scared of his shadow, the shadow boxing would have to stop, sooner rather than later.

"Let me put it another way to you, Buddha," the Dong suggested, lining up the Buddha and, after baiting him as might a banderillero from Bilbao, prepared to skewer him in the manner of a masterful matador, taunting him further before stepping in for the kill.

What ambush is this? The Buddha considered the safety of his companions and his own naivety, before thinking fleetingly of Dilly Dalai and Bang Ki-Moon, shuddering at calculations of any treachery on their part. Whatever the Dong sought, it wasn't any advice from the Buddha of Ballyhuppahaun. This was a man consumed, where compassion had surrendered to the sadness in his soul many moons ago.

The Dong prompted again, harder now: "The Mojo of Mayo, Buddha, remember him? Or do I need to ring a bell to bring you out of your meditation, or wherever it is you've gone on me?"

Remember him? How could the Buddha ever forget. He would forever be haunted by the ghastly sight of the gaunt, ghostly figure, hanging pale-green-faced from the bow of the willow on the banks of the Moy, his tongue protruding between his deathly purple lips, near matching the colour of his robes.

"The Mojo, a decent and holy man – nay, a saintly man. My third cousin through marriage on my mother's side and you stab him in the back and leave him for dead, Buddha. Just how is a king to stomach that?"

The Dong could not throw a stick without hitting some cousin or other it seemed, but, with his back to the wall, the Buddha thought better than to jest.

"It is true what you say, all-seeing sovereign. I have been afflicted with the knowledge of the ages, but through no skulduggery or blackguarding. For sure, I trekked the Emerald Isle in the service of the Mojo, season in and out, in search of the breadan feasa, the legendary and elusive salmon of knowledge. To his misfortune and mine, I did hook the fish unawares, twenty-one years into our quest. It looked like any other I had caught and cooked, a delicacy exclusively dished up to the Dong's unfortunate cousin. While roasting on the spit, the skin of the fish blistered due to a wind-fanned flame. The Mojo was furious and instructed me to burst the bubbles along the salmon's spine. I did so with my left thumb, scalding it and only by chance stuck it in my gob to suck and ease the stinging pain. In so doing was I first, by pure fluke, to eat the crispy skin of the salmon of knowledge and strike an accord with the Tuatha Dé Danann, as had been ordained."

"The curse of seven bad marriages on you," spat the Dong bitterly, upon hearing the tale. But in the unlikely event of such marriages occurring, the Buddha could live with that. The truth had proved the Buddha's trump card. Checkmate.

CHAPTER V

The Dreamtime

'I can't seem to face up to the facts.
I'm tense and nervous and I... can't relax.
I can't sleep, cause my bed's on fire.
Don't touch me I'm a real live wire.'

The Buddha loved the dreamtime. The minute he hit the scratcher, he was out for the count before his head touched the pillow. Sweet dreams. It had always been this way. He would sleep like a log, then awaken slowly from his slumber and start each day with a new song in his heart. Not anymore.

He had heard of nightmares but never known them. Now he seemed to know little else, as they lingered on to haunt his waking hours and pounce on every moment he set aside. The Buddha was in a bad place and he did not need any kahuna, monk, witch or surfer to tell him that he would have to get to the bottom of his night-time torment before he would be free to travel on.

No matter how far, or in what direction, he went in his dreamscapes, he could always see the Twin Towers of Power, sometimes lurking over his shoulder, sometimes sitting on the horizon. All along the watchtowers, the prisoners kept a view. The Dong had decided to post only spies, slaves and sleveens as lookouts. They were forced to live on meagre rations and could only return to the mainstream – and to the freedom of the citadel – if they captured or intercepted an enemy of the Dongdom or its allies. They in turn could opt to work the watchtowers, or, as an unsavoury alternative, they would be hung out to dry.

An arching sign spanned the gates to the citadel proclaiming: Work Will Set You Free. Each week the slaving workers would build yet another vast city, every brick and plaster painted white to protect them from the searing sun – the White Cities of Babylon. Scorching sun or not, the workers never stopped moving and, like machine cogs, they built another concrete jungle by degrees; a bar code of Roman numerals tattooed into the backs of their burnt necks.

By dark it rained a lot, but the Buddha could see no crops, no vegetables and no flowers. When he went to cook his morning and evening meals, he searched inside his satchel for food and ingredients, finding nothing but salt. Lots of salt. Sifting through the worn corners of the bag, out of each side it would pour like fine sand in an hourglass egg timer. This sensation had even put him off his usual two soft-boiled googies in the mornings. His wok was also missing. A woman he knew but could not put a face on would always remark: "Wok gone walkabout, then?"

People scurried left and right in search of water, but as they held their vessels to the heavens to harvest the incessant downpour, it transpired that they had produced only sieves and colanders.

This would torment the Buddha as he slept, and every time he would reach again for his wok to help trap the rain, only to be taunted further by bitter mosquitoes sent to remind him that, next time, he should take care to bring a vessel – one that was not so holey.

As he wondered what to do, he wandered on an aimless walkabout, meeting people he knew so well but whose names he could never recall in time to address them properly. When he had passed by, their names would come tripping off his tongue, but as he doubled back to display some civility, they were gone.

Then there were those he had never met before but was certain he had known all his life. Their names were easy to remember and he would stop and chat to Aung San Suu Kyi as she knitted a funny hat from all the colours of the rainbow. Sitting beside her on the rugged stone wall was Tin Oo, the tinker. As fast as he could manage, he was mending pots and pans, plugging their holes and passing out the repaired utensils to those walking by.

All the people in the line were coloured. The Buddha was the only Caucasian. By the time he realised this, he also noticed that he was the only one walking in the opposite direction. He was not sure if this was what Bengal the Hare had whispered in his ear, or did he say something different every time? He could never remember once he awoke. Much and all as he prepared to wake and recall every detail, his dream defied him time and time again.

Strongmen would march past, big black men with bulging biceps and strong stomachs. They seemed fit to carry anything and they held heavy canoes, currachs and kayaks shoulder high, seemingly unaware of the load they were lumbering, as they made it look effortless. They were followed by stunning, buxom women wearing lei and (like the men) little else.

Out of amber eyes set in pearl, they stared at the Buddha but said nothing before looking away. The Buddha was always surprised and could never fathom why they never had any children with them.

The walls were sprayed with slogans and graffiti. It often varied, with emblazoned emblems, symbols and logos that the Buddha had never seen before. They read: "Four legs good, two legs bad." And: "Everyone is equal, but some are more equal than others." These signs had the numbers 1 9 8 4 written after them. Another line read: "In Lilliput, size matters", followed in this case by the numbers 1 7 2 6. The slogans were invariably written in red.

Much more striking were the seven colours of the rainbow, which spanned the jagged walls from top to bottom, while scribbled inside its arch was the line: "You can't stop the waves, but you can learn to surf." As the Buddha was already an accomplished surfer, this was even more perplexing.

No matter which direction the Buddha looked – whether north, east, west or south – the news was always the same, as the shadow of the Twin Towers of Power hung over him, its watchdogs in their watchtowers burning holes in his back even as he faced them.

At last then, familiar faces. The mammoths traipsed past, peering from amber irises set in red eye sockets. They had plenty to tell and much to say, but although they chose to remain silent, made sure to turn their heads until they caught the Buddha eye-to-eye. They then looked away, gazing down as they marched on.

The Buddha too was stunned to silence by these familiar but unfriendly faces. He knew each and every one by name, but as he called out his voice rang hollow and not one of the mammoths looked back, even though there were lots of them.

This was like rubbing salt in the wound to the Buddha, who could not bear it. He no longer trudged but broke into a brisk walk, before long a jog and then an all-out gallop as fast as he could. He was frantic, desperate to get away, to escape the peering eyes of the long line of people, the lookouts from the Towers and the lumbering mammoths with their calves in tow.

Fast now, faster than he had ever managed to make it in real life. Everything that passed at this pace was but a blur. At breakneck speed, the Buddha looked back and, in a whirlwind, everything and everyone he had passed along the way was caught up in a storm, tossed and tumbling all round him in a terrific twister. Consternation and carnage rained from the sky; bits and pieces of people, broken limbs and fractured boats, the bulk of shaggy elephants shooting through the air like flimsy kites. Their tusks came flying separately, stabbing, sticking and gouging mercilessly as they passed, showing no favour to man, woman or beast, excepting the Buddha, the only one not taken into the tornado. Tangled up, beaten blue, he stopped running and stood fast, as the last of the maelstrom thundered past, leaving only silence in its wake.

Not even the scores of eyes along the watchtower dared blink or draw a heavy breath. They had a bird's eye view. They had watched from the best vantage point in the whole world as the Buddha's nightmare unfolded. Without any conniving, they reached the same conclusion: they would never speak of this saga; it would not earn them their freedom. They had been about many towns and met too many wide-eyed messengers, wet behind the ears. Instead, they tucked into their nosebags – nothing special, but any respite would do.

The Buddha was awake, his deadly dream banished by the dawn. He wiped away the tears and called out to Dodo, wondering once again as to why he had appeared to abandon him. Countless times this dream had taunted and tested him, but never did Dodo feature, and never once had he come to his aid.

He gave thanks that it was, after all, only a dream, and that the nighttime tsunami of torment had ended. The minute his feet hit the ground beneath the hammock, he realised just how hungry he really was.

Chapter VI

The Sport of Kings

'I'm not singing for the future
I'm not dreaming of the past
I'm not talking of the first time
I never think about the last.'

The crowds at Ballybrit were claustrophobic. Crowds were present that it had taken weeks on end to assemble. It would be a long road back, but no matter, everyone here loved to gamble. It could be said that the gathering at Ballybrit was one big gamble. The tented city teemed with a tarlike beverage, which foamed and frothed as it fermented. Big Brother Brew, or BBB as it was known to its legion of fans, was a firm favourite at the festival. Favourites also were tarts, hot steaming tarts, best eaten with custard, but also fancied with cream and washed down with a big slug of BBB. These were the heady days of the sport of kings and Ballybrit was its climax. The crowds delightedly danced and dallied in this canvas city.

From plastic beakers those assembled imbibed the brew, sipped champagne, sucked snails from their shells and sang ballads of bold adventures. The hoi polloi rubbed shoulders with the rich and famous, the ruling elite, Les Congestez. It was great. This was as good as it gets. Great fun for friend and farmer, prince and pauper and every race, colour and creed was here. No one who was anyone missed out on Ballybrit; its tented city was the capital of culture, the cultural capital, agri-culture, sub-culture and capital culture for the great and the good and mere mortals.

Everyone flocked to be at the races. No one wanted it said of them that they were not at the races. A flock of seagulls flew past, narrowly missing a crowd of Yahoos with their aerial bombardment. They had been startled by the arrival in hot air balloons of dapper, dandy and dainty dignitaries. The crowds stared in awe, puzzled as to how those bulbous balloons managed to defy gravity and stay afloat, full to the gills of the rich and famous.

The Buddha fumed and flayed around, wondering as to the futility of his presence. He lost Dodo again in the milieu and had yet to catch a glimpse of the fabled nags with their funny names – the likes of Paddy the Plasterer, Joe the Plumber and Bob the Builder, Catch Me If You Can. There was no sign of a single mare and it was all too intense for the Buddha. Out of the corner of his eye, he copped yet another flock – this time of sheep – on an adjacent slope. If he could only nobble Dodo right now, he would elope to the slope and plot a route back to Ballyhuppahaun, but just like in a bad dream, Dodo was nowhere to be found.

Buddha dithered around, a denizen in a daze. He was in a different time zone, light years away. Everyone on earth, and even further afield, seemed to be here. The Dong had promised, while press-ganging him to come along, that he would give him a banker and explain everything to him. This place had a language all of its own. Sign language, with strange men in hats signalling to other strange men in hats, who looked at them through large lenses, before putting down the goggles and gesticulating back.

Then there were bankers, favourites, outsiders, fillies, long shots, short odds, odds on, odd people, sure things, nags, bets and hedging bets, dead certs, three-card-tricks, shams and beours. The Buddha's mind boggled. He was banjaxed.

Just then, and by chance, he spotted Dodo. That dunce, he thought, yet unable to suppress a smile as he clocked Dodo, his face stuck to a tuft of pink-purple candyfloss, as if he was trying to eat a large, fluffy albino rabbit upside down.

Everyone else seemed to be really enjoying themselves but the Buddha, alas, just wasn't at the races.

CHAPTER VII

Water, water, everywhere

'I'm gonna make a change,
For once in my life
It's gonna feel real good,
Gonna make a difference
Gonna make it right...'

There was more to the Twin Towers of Power than meets the eye. Quite literally, it was one gargantuan drill bit, burrowing towards the centre of the earth. In simple terms, the Dongdom was using more water than it could mine or manufacture. The King, perhaps a knave but not a fool, realised early on in his rule that he would have to find more water. He did have some, but much of it was stinking, salty or manky with mosquitoes. Suitable solutions to the problem had so far evaded his greatest scientists. In secret labs, he enslaved them, with albatrosses tethered to their necks to help them concentrate on the urgency of their endeavours.

He kept them apart and unaware of another crew that he had put up in a penthouse suite in the east wing of the castle. If the scientists were getting the stick – and the wrong end of it to boot, he secretly chuckled – then this shower were certainly on the carrot. They assured the Dong that they could change wine into water and, as the Dongdom was coming down with grapes, this was worth a shot. Far-fetched, the King admitted to himself with a snigger, but you had to admire their gumption and, after all, if they double-crossed him he would roast them one by one on a spit and have their guts for garters. No sour grapes.

The Dong knew his loyal subjects were a thirsty bunch, but without water, they would become bloodthirsty. Not even Les Congestez could be relied upon if push came to shove. All this construction work put a further strain on supplies, as man and machines required more aqua. Once it rained, his reign was secure, thirsts were quenched and contraptions cooled, for all his engineers and advisers had yet to successfully devise a manner or means of safely securing a reserve of drinking water. While so far at a loss, he had already decided that once they had conceived a way of safely storing drinking water from the rains and snow that fell, he would ingeniously label it a 'reservoir'. If the gamble of the colossal borehole to the middle of the earth did not pay off, they would merely use up their supply of water faster and hasten the demise not alone of the Dongdom but all who dwelled therein. In between times, there would of course be hell to pay.

To this end, the Dong had summoned the Buddha from Ballyhuppahaun. If he was indeed all knowing and all seeing, perhaps he had managed a manner to appease the heavens and secure water. If not, he was well travelled – if not well heeled – and surely certain to know the whereabouts of supplies of fresh water, enough even to buy some time until the giant drill did its bit.

The Buddha was the Dong's joker in the pack. The Dong wasn't a good gambler; he was a great gambler – not to mention a sore loser – and this Buddha would not trump him when it came to life and death, as by Jesus he was no Mojo to be found hanging limply from a tree. No, the Buddha would swing first, if needs be. He was, after all, a constant gardener. He would sicken you with tales of cabbage, courgettes and coriander. He was friends too with the wily witches of Świętokrzyski, who, according to all his latest report, had locks of fresh water, as if by some divine right.

Down the years, the Dong dispatched shoals of scouts and spies in search of fresh water sources, but all in vain. Most did not return, while those that did had little in the line of good news. Whenever this occurred, the Dong duly dispatched them on another journey from which they did not return. The heads of these messengers were preserved and impaled on the city walls. The Dong knew that one day he would have to go to war for water but, in order to fund this war, there would have to be water. He needed to know for sure before he waged war again.

There had been, in the past, the Seven-Day War – a mere skirmish and warm-up for the real thing. That Holy War was a blockbuster. The Dongdom lost more souls then than during the bubonic plague. It was one hell of a war that sent them straight to heaven. How it had cleansed the spirit of sin and the soil of shams, instilling a new appreciation in his subjects for the simple things in life. Then, of course, there was the Thousand-Year War, which had fallen to him to finish off. That was a sweet crusade and who would now dare to doubt or cross the Dong?

As he reflected, the Dong knew all too well that for another war he would have to prepare well, and then prepare to win. He had a cunning plan, but first he had to find just cause, find water worth fighting for. This would be no dogfight; this would be a great war, a war to end all wars. It would be the mother and father of all wars. If only he could confirm there was water, there would be war. He had hoped to avoid this bloodshed by rationing and regulating water supply but the King's two top advisors had cautioned against this, as he would, they argued, become immensely unpopular, leading to riots, anarchy and total chaos. So, war it would have to be. The King would choose the lesser of two evils, for the common good.

CHAPTER VIII

The Writing is on the Wall

'What about sunrise
What about rain
What about all the things
That you said we were to gain.
What about killing fields
Is there a time
What about all the things
That you said was yours and mine.
Did you ever stop to notice
All the blood we've shed before
Did you ever stop to notice
The crying Earth, the weeping shores?'

There probably was a time when the Dong slept soundly, but he just couldn't remember when. He did not believe in dreams or nightmares, for they did not apply to him. Each night, he'd lay wide awake, eyes wide shut. Sleeping was a waste of time. He tired of sleep; it was not for kings. Above the head of his bed, engraved in thick oak panels was the code of conduct, the motto of his beloved Republican Guard: All for One, One for All, Everyone for Themselves. It was their esprit de corps and had served them well, ever since the Dong had taken charge after the untimely and unexpected death of his father. As a mark of respect to his father and the gods, it was strictly forbidden to mutter or mention his name.

In place of dreaming, the Dong allowed his mind to wander, as it helped mark off the hours of darkness. Often, his thoughts would drift to Zako, his best, loyal and trusted friend. If Zako were not his brother, Dong would want him to be. Although they were not raised together, they had always thought and fought as one. He remembered, with no small measure of pride and pleasure, the day of their rite-of-passage, when they were accepted into the corps.

For his challenge, Zako had captured a stunningly beautiful, translucent blue Morphidae butterfly in the Amazing Forest. In its prime, he carefully and gently wrapped it in the softest of snow-white tissue, before setting it slowly alight with a burning twig taken from the smouldering campfire. The Dong had been impressed beyond words.

For his own task, the Dong set out on a dangerous quest to find a rare species of goldfish. After camping out night after night on many different islands, and after going to great pains for 365 days, he finally struck gold, capturing a specimen six-inch goldfish in Lough Corrib, near Cong. The Dong was elated as he returned home with his prize. His father would be pleased. Zako would be surprised.

Back in the heart of the empire, the Dong waited for weeks until he had a complete and captive audience. Once he had, and with his bare hands, he fetched the goldfish from the bulbous globe bowl and placed it carefully on the flecked terrazzo marble floor, watching its first flaps, gasps and gulps at close quarters. The Dong had then retired to wine and dine and bask in the delight that warmed him to this very day. The spectacle went on for weeks as the crowd by turns feverishly applauded or watched in stunned silence. After forty days and forty nights, the fish stopped trying to catch a breath and just lay there with its mouth open.

As a show of respect, the Dong had it preserved and mounted above his bed, next to the motto. At the wall near the foot of the four-poster was a massive, floor-length mirror, rivalled only by a matching mirror mounted on the ceiling, placed there so that the King could see the goldfish from all angles. Although always regarded as invaluable and a sign of good fortune, from that day onwards goldfish were even rarer and priceless. Only the extremely exalted, wealthy or powerful could wear a goldfish. Their capture remained a closely guarded secret and they were stuffed by the most skilful taxidermists in the land. Then, they could be worn as a symbol of status and strength.

The Dong was the only person known to have four, not counting the one in the silver embossed glass case above his bed. Each one had its own story to tell – the bracelet, the necklace and the earrings, which were only ever worn on special occasions of state, or on the eve of battle. As the Dong stared, unblinking, into the eyes of the goldfish in the case, the first rays of the daylight glanced off the glass. Good, he thought, building would resume on the Tower at first light. There was no time to waste. Water was, after all, worth its weight in gold. No time to sleep – what a waste of time.

CHAPTER IX

The Rainbow Gathering

'Those who feel the breath of sadness
Sit down next to me
Those who find they're touched by madness
Sit down next to me
Those who find themselves ridiculous
Sit down next to me
Love, in fear, in hate, in tears.'

The Buddha never missed the annual Rainbow Gathering. Now, he looks on as a young woman with braided blonde hair rode a pony, bareback, across the camp, chased by screeching, barefoot children and skinny, black-and-white barking dogs. Smoke wafts in the damp morning air, drifting out across the heather, the forest and the mountains that surround and shelter this secluded site. There is a cacophony of other noises – singing, talking, and laughter, the chopping of sticks, the fast-flowing river dipping over the rocks, sounding horns and – always – the incessant and infectious rhythm of djembe drums.

The camp circle is set out by imposing tee pees, mostly off-white but with many others as colourful as the Rainbow Nation. Dotted between, above and below them, a maze of motley tents sit all across the plain, snuggled right up against the valley's easy slopes of the Slieve Bloom Mountains. This spectacular, sprawling encampment at Ballyhuppahaun is the latest gathering of the Rainbow Nation.

'The Rainbow' is the name given to the gathering of a growing band of loosely affiliated travellers and tribes, united in the common bond of respect for Mother Earth, the elements, ecology, creation and nature. Variously labelled as hippies, new age travellers, good lifers and dinosaurs, the group members themselves prefer the term, if one must be used, 'Rainbow People'.

"You can call us what you want, but I call it messin' with the kid," the Buddha would joke to newcomers, scaring them half out of their wits with his take on Rory Gallagher – a disturbing leap and thrashing air guitar.

The gathering is bewildering, bizarre and beautiful, the days and nights as colourful as the collection of creatures and creeds found amid this organised chaos. The Rainbow Travellers are from everywhere and from nowhere. The campsite is a hive of activity throughout the day and, while there are no leaders, a strict code is observed. Two basic devices maintain order: the 'Talking Stick' and the 'Magic Hat'.

As all the decisions are reached by consensus, there are regular 'councils' or 'circles'. The 'Talking Stick' is passed clockwise, giving the speaker the floor, each in turn voicing their opinion until a consensus is reached – an arrangement that seems close to the ultimate democratic process. The 'Magic Hat' is the communal way of providing for food and sustenance, with everyone contributing according to their means, based on mutual trust and respect. If it runs out, everyone goes without.

The gathering operates on 'Rainbow time', meaning that two communal meals are served daily when the food is ready, prepared in four busy cooperative kitchens. Mealtime is signalled by the sounding of a conch. The meals themselves comprise simple, nourishing salads, sprouts, porridge, fruit and unleavened Chapatti bread. There is a special play area and kitchen for the children, where more regular and less spicy food is prepared, while there is a constant supply of herbal teas from the Chai kitchen, where the Buddha was usually to be found.

The Rainbow People may be unorganised, but they are in no way disorganised. The gathering comes equipped with its own library; gravity-based hot shower system, a children's play area (with an ingenious popcorn device) and a sweat lodge, before which users are required to fast and meditate.

Bathing is only permitted downstream in the Owenass River, which cuts through the camp. Utensils are never washed in the river but in the water drawn from it. There is not a speck of dirt or debris, which, for the Buddha, comes just in time, helping him to de-stress from the distress of the littered Dongdom and its butt-strewn streets.

"This is not a 'festival', as 'festival' suggests that you pay for something and that somebody else is responsible for providing the entertainment and activity. Here, everybody is responsible for themselves and nothing happens unless we make it happen," explains the Buddha, welcoming the excited Dodo to his first Rainbow. "If something is left undone one day, everyone makes sure it is done twice as well the next day. That's the basic, co-operative philosophy of the gathering," Buddha adds, grateful for the sights that greet the weary pair under a rainbow arch proclaiming, 'Welcome Home'.

Latrines dug in the earth are located way up on the heathered slopes. Later, when it comes time to move on, they will be back-filled, restored and planted over with a scattering of bluebells, snowdrops, cowslips and primroses.

"The gathering is a healing time for us and the earth. There is a lot of energy and a strong spiritual aspect. We are not getting together in a hedonistic way, but in a healing way. It's very easy to lose ourselves in the TV and fridge, so when we come to Rainbow we lay ourselves a bit more naked," says Martin from the South of England, with a warm hug for his old pals, the Buddha and Dodo.

Time stands still in the Rainbow gathering, its inhabitants oblivious of the stresses and pressures of modern living, drawing much of their influences and rituals from the Native American, Celtic and Indian customs. All over the camp, people participate in workshops on everything from yoga, juggling, meditation, chanting, re-birthing and 'focalizing', to making beaded jewellery and playing the Australian didgeridoo. Others just relax, or dance, sing and join in the beating of the bongo, bodhráns, congos and tom-tom drums.

The anthem of the Rainbow People rings long into the night: "The river is flowing, flowing and growing, the river is flowing back to the sea. Mother Earth shall carry me, a child I will always be, and Mother Earth shall carry me, back to the sea. The moon she is waiting, waxing and waning, the moon she is waiting for us to be free. Sister Moon watch over me, a child I shall always be, Sister Moon watch over me, until we are free."

The beating of drums drives others on to dance in the dark for hour upon hour, some of them in an Amazon tribal dance in which they will not stop until dawn. Music from the tents and tee pees is non-stop. Instruments from all over the world are played, while the songs cover everything from Chicago jazz and blues to the ethnic folk songs of Bombay and Brazil. At night, the outskirts of the camp are practically pitch black. What light there is comes from candles or the odd torch. Some choose to sit and share ideas around fires in talking circles. The principal gathering is found at the centre of the camp, around the fire pit that forms the symbolic hub for the main circle, which is set out in the form of a Celtic cross or medicine wheel. Like fireflies, the assembled faces glow with light from the flames, while only a foot or two away, the night remains inky black.

Conversations range across everything from the dangers of intruding media, astrology, and the warm welcome the visitors had received in Ireland, to global warming, the Dalai Lama and the quality of the previous night's drumming – which, it was generally agreed, was better than the best entertainment from the top hi-tech London clubs.

Out of the darkness, a young man approaches the gathering's notice board. Mostly, it caters for requests for lifts to places like Spain, England, Morocco, Dublin and Feile in Thurles. Among these requests however, someone has written, in thick black marker, 'What is this, the chosen few? Are we not all equal?' Anxious to reply in the wee hours of the morning, the man borrows a pen and writes, 'Not the chosen few, but the few that have chosen!' "Now I can go asleep," he says, skinny and sallow, shorts slinking from his bony, not-a-pick-on-him hips as he slips into the night. "Out of the mouths of babes," mused the Buddha, who had been watching the event unfold. He was amused, and his only fear for the feisty scribe was that he would disappear into one of the rare cracks of light from a kite lantern, which occasionally beamed out across the grass.

The Buddha loved the Rainbow. He always made a special effort to make it to the gatherings but he would never forget his first. Each time back now was like a first visit again. Renewing, recharging, reviewing, regrouping, re-energising and realising. The gathering was where he first met Grażyna and the other witches. In the beginning, he remembered feeling the trepidation of the new and unknown, before uneasiness at the mystery, madness and mayhem all melted away, mesmerising in the magical quality of a whisper, waking him up to what really matters.

At the Full Moon Party that July, he and Grażyna had held hands for the first time. The drummers drove the night delirious; the flames from the campfires danced along; the kite lanterns, like fireflies, flimsily but gamely challenged the milky night sky. We all held hands and afterwards ate cakes – the best-ever cáca milis reserved for such occasions; ring-a-ring-a-rosy round in circles we went, holding hands with whoever came and joined in the circle, lost in the stars and the songs. So happy. Silly happy. Silly happy and just holding hands.

"Earth my body; Water my blood; Air my breath and Fire my spirit."

"Tierrra mi cuerpo; Agua mi sangre; Aire mi aliento y Fuego mi espiritu."

Surfers, soulmates, Rainbow revellers, travellers and warriors all, we sang out our songs, childish smiles on our faces, howling at the moon. So happy. Silly happy.

All that was changed now though, changed utterly. "A terrible beauty is born," said the Buddha, when Dodo had first come to him with the gossip. Still groggy and stiff after sleeping twenty to a tee pee, the Buddha nonetheless liked bandying around a bit of verse. While the Yeats sounding-off was wasted on Dodo, the Buddha proclaimed that the real peril was failing to ever love. "Love poetry," he hastened to add, "as without poetry you perish".

"Poetry is, after all, the yoga of the soul, as arithmetic is of the mind. How can you ever expect your soul to display any posture if you don't learn – and I mean learn to love and love to learn – poetry?" the Buddha asked, finishing with a flourish. Dodo, now more bewildered and baffled than when he first arrived at the tee pee village, persisted nevertheless with the pressing matter of the gossip.

"Wagging tongues, Dodo, are as harmless as a dog's wagging tail: merely looking for attention, a treat or a pat on the head. Sticks-and-stones and all that. It'd be more in your line to have our breakfast ready, instead of spreading idle gossip, and us with waves to catch, songs to sing and miles to go before we sleep. Write that one down," ordered the Buddha, who was on a roll.

Despite the levity however, the Buddha was privately perplexed. Weeks earlier, he had spotted Granard, Graigue, Gort, Gurteen, Grallagh, Graffa and Gortnahoo, along with their ringleader, Garrysallagh, arrive at the gathering. Garrysallagh could be dirty (that was his form), but as he and the Buddha had never been friends or fans, there was no loss there. How many times had the Buddha spelled out to Dodo the warning that, if it walks like a duck, and looks like a duck, then it must be...trouble. "Trouble, trouble, I'm trying to chase trouble but it's chasing me. Trouble, trouble, trouble with a capital 'T'," the Buddha intoned, humming the Horslips to himself. He always hummed or paced, elephant-like, from one foot to the other when he was bothered and uneasy, a habit that usually ended up making everyone around him more nervous than himself, and he preaching calm.

Garrysallagh and his gang of Gryposaurus were not the problem though. The Pterosaurs from Portlaoise, along with Portadown, Pollaphuca, Portarlington, Portumna, Pollrone, and that pismire Portnashangan had all flown in for this gathering, after no sign of them for years. For good measure, their boneheaded cousin, Pullagh the Pachycephalosaurus, to which they were all practically related, had also shown up.

Reputed to have brains to burn, the Stegosaurus clan must have done just that. Shrone, Shrule, Sheskin, Stookane, Shinrone, Skreen, Slemish, Slieve Mish, Slievenamon, Slieveroe, Slievenamuck, Shallon and Sleveen would have no problem stringing you along, stringing you up, skinning you and coming back for the hide. No place or point in the Buddha reciting poetry, prose or Proust, nor looking for succour of any sort from those guys.

Still, all was not lost. The cool Tyrannosaurus clan were also out in force. The T-Rex boys had a bark worst than their bite and they'd always give you a fair hearing. Tallaght, Tonregee, Taughboyne, Tavanagh, Tiknock, Timahoe, Tirconnell, Tinnakill, Torc, Tomfinlough, Toberbilly, Tobbereendoney, Tobercurry and Tuam, who were all well travelled, were not a bad bunch to have in your corner if it came to a showdown. One of their ilk though, Toomyvara, could not be trusted if push came to shove in a public place.

Then there was the Dromesaurs, who received a rapturous reaction when they arrived for the Full Moon Party. They were a formidable bunch if they got their claws into you. But again, no harm, no foul, and if you were straight up with Dangandargan, Doonane, Dalkey, Deelish and Dublin, Dernish, Derry, Derryduff, Derryfada, Derrydorragh, Derrylahan, Derrylea, Derrylough, Derrymore, Donegal, Donnybrook and Donneycarney, Dingle, Dangan and Doonooney.

There were two other clans who could not be taken for granted, and how they sided in the inevitably impending confrontation between the Rainbow way and the Dong despotism would prove significant – even decisive. The Carcharodontosaurus clan and the Brontosaurus bunch were heavyweights, giants among men and could not be treated lightly.

Buddha knew full well that he had brushed some of the Brontosaurus up the wrong way. Ballinasloe wasn't backward in coming forward and filling the Buddha in on the clan's misgivings over his carry-on. Ballina, Ballinagar, Ballinmona, Ballincollig, Ballinalack, Ballinakill, Ballinspittle, Ballintubbert, Baltinglass, Blessington, Ballygowan, Ballyheige, Ballybay, Ballinwully, Ballytore, Ballybough, Ballybunion, Ballycolla, Ballyporeen, Ballykelly, Ballymena, Ballyea, and even Ballybeg, Ballinamought and Ballydehob had put on the poor mouth and given him down the banks.

According to Ballinasloe, who the Buddha had perhaps unwisely opined as being well named, only Baltinglass and Blessington of the Brontosaurus brethern had butted in on his behalf. There was also Ballyhooly, who believed that the Buddha was merely retelling the tapestry of his travels "and sure what harm in that," she had reckoned, sticking her neck out. She was known to be fond of a good time and her view was promptly dismissed. Not leaving anything to chance, the rumour mill ground out a version of events that even had her fancying the Buddha, and, so besotted, who could be bothered paying Ballyhooly a blind bit of heed? Indeed.

The problem with the Buddha, as Dodo had heard first-hand from the Gathering's Chai kitchen, was that he had gotten too big for his boots and needed to be taken down a peg or two. The protagonists were seemingly unaware of Dodo's apprenticeship to the Buddha.

"Is that so?" The Buddha had practically snarled this after Dodo had come running once more with the tittle-tattle. "You know how I prefer to go barefoot," Buddha added, regretting both the anger that was stirring inside him and the facetiousness of his remark the moment he had muttered it. In a bid to make amends, the Buddha proposed a stroll through the Slieve Blooms, along the banks of blooming heather and furze.

The hazy day had brought the midges out in force and they'd eat you alive if it wasn't for the swallows. Smoky sandlewood at suppertime would keep the midges at bay this evening, but for now, the nuisance was a small price to pay. The pair pressed on over Lacken Lane, which hid a secret spring well — too good a thirst-dousing opportunity to let pass by. As they cut across the back of Rosenallis and made tracks for a swim in the Catholes, by chance they encountered Johnny the Fox and Jimmy the Weed and them in the unlikely company of Joe Milis. "Two quare hawks if there ever were," Buddha adjudged, mentoring Dodo after they were out of earshot, without wasting his wit on the two. "If it walks like a duck...," said Dodo. The Buddha laughed, Dodo being as right as rain.

Later, sprawled out on the grassy slope beneath his favourite Wollemi Pine, the Buddha took the opportunity to explain where he was coming from to Dodo. He resorted, as was his wont, to the teachings of the Zen masters. Once the Buddha mentioned the teacher Hakuin, he didn't have to ask for Dodo's undivided attention a second time.

"The Zen master Hakuin was praised by his neighbours as one living a pure life. The story goes that a beautiful Japanese girl, whose parents owned a food store, lived near him. Suddenly, and without any warning, her parents discovered she was pregnant.

"This made her parents angry. She would not confess who the man was, but after much harassment eventually named Hakuin. In great anger, the parents went to the master and levelled their accusation. 'Is that so?' was all he would say.

"After the child was born it was brought to Hakuin. By this time, he had lost his reputation, which did not trouble him, but he took very good care of the child. He obtained milk from his neighbours and everything else the little one needed. A year later, the girl-mother could stand it no longer. She told her parents the truth, that the real father of the child was a young man who worked in the fishmarket.

"The mother and father of the girl went at once to Hakuin to beg his forgiveness, to apologise at length, and to get the child back again. Hakuin was willing. In yielding the child, all he said was, 'Is that so?'

"Now, what's for supper?" the Buddha uttered suddenly, in what was more of an order than an enquiry. He was as wily a survivor as the old Wollemi tree.

Back at Ballyhuppahaun, the Buddha opted for a meal with Dodo, Gee and a few of her colourful companions from the Tatras. They included Vishal from Mauritius, Marcia from Rio, Xan and Ivan from Galicia, Hippy Bill, Lanky his dog and The Legend from Lettermacaward. The bard's son would link up lovely with Doolin for a few fireside tunes. Who knows who else would blow in on the wind and there would be plenty on the pot for stragglers. There were no strangers in Ballyhuppahaun.

The evening called for a one-pot wonder, a feed for friends, perhaps even that special vegetable moussaka recipe the Buddha had wrangled from the kitchen of the Mighty Jim, the most famous chef to hail from the foothills of the Slieve Blooms. "Winner alright," the Buddha declared, licking his lips. He never gambled when it came to grub.

Aubergine, red and green lentils, onion, garlic, mushrooms, chickpeas, tomatoes, eggs, yoghurt, Parmesan cheese, herbs, salt and pepper were all assembled, before the Buddha demonstrated his culinary skills to the Dodo, as the guests arrived and the conversation, good humour and music flowed. Just thinking and talking about the food made the Buddha hungry but his famished guests would have to wait a while for this Mount Rath masterpiece. As he began, he addressed those assembled with evident relish.

"Place the lentils, vegetable stock and bouquet garni in a saucepan, bring to the boil and cook for about twenty minutes. You can always add more water if needs be. After this, drain and keep to one side.

"Fry the onion and garlic in olive oil, then stir in the mushrooms onto the pan and toss around for a few minutes before adding in the cooked lentils, followed by the chick peas, tomatoes, tomato puree. Then season with salt and pepper. Still with me?" the Buddha asked, glancing up. He sure loved to show off in the kitchen.

"Bring to the boil and then simmer for about fifteen minutes, before again setting to one side. The aubergines should now be placed in a flat roasting tray. Season and then drizzle with olive oil before frying them.

"Now lay it all out with love in a dish. First, a layer of aubergines on the bottom, then spread on some of the lentil and chickpea mixture and continue until all the aubergine and lentil mix is used. Finally, beat the yoghurt, egg and some salt and pepper together, before spreading over the top of the last layer of aubergines. Sprinkle with the cheese and place in a hot oven. Cook until it's ready."

Tom Petty and the Heartbreakers, along with some surfers, had joined the swollen supper circle, as the wafting smells had signalled the impending banquet. "You don't have to live like a refugee," strummed out the Guru and the Kiwi. Somehow, the djembe drummers in the far field managed to beat out a percussion chorus in perfect tempo. The Shagmire had already made his move and hunkered down next to the witches. He broached the possibility of a holiday in Cambodia. The healing powers of herbs and wild flowers were doing the rounds when Zulu, Killer and Nobby sauntered in. This troika made some nervous and Nobby's 12-inch blade, dangling from his left hip, didn't help. Luckily, though, these boys were as decent as the day is long and so no one knew how Killer got his name. He was a horse wrangler who wouldn't harm a fly. The constellations glittered far above; very few night skies beat Ballyhuppahaun. There was talk of a football match with the natives and plans for a totem pole hatched.

The witches seized the opportunity to round up volunteers to build a sweat lodge the next morning. Shagmire was first with his hand up, much to the amusement of his fellow surfers. "A leopard never changes its stripes," the Guru averred. "Make that spots," corrected Tom Petty, after which the Guru spent a gruelling night explaining that he was referring to no one in particular. "I simply meant that people will never let you down. If you allow that they will always behave as you expect, you won't be disappointed. It's like the scorpion and the frog…oh I give up. I'm wasting my time," protested the Guru, hands out, pleading for support.

"I thought that made a lot of sense," said Zulu soberly, coming to the rescue. It was too late, however. Runner and Snag (two surfer buddies of the Guru) were in convulsions. "Throwing pearls to swine," Killer remarked as he took sides, but his interjection only made matters worse, as Runner and Snag were joined by Biker in suggesting there had been too much sweet cake doing the rounds. "Too much sweet cake, cáca milis. Too much sugar," judged Biker, who then proceeded to produce a massive menu from some posh hotel out of his haversack, before summoning the Buddha.

"I digress for a moment, master, and dance delicately on your big toes, merely to beg the question – as reluctant as I am to freefall and languish in hyperbole – when, in the name of I-can't-say-in-front-of-the-children, will dinner ever be served? We're all bloody well starving!"

Biker got his name because when he walked, he was always leaning over to one side, as if he was going around a corner on a motorbike. In this split second, the supper circle, which by then had expanded to two facing circles, had all gone silent at once. Now, everyone just erupted in whoops, cheers and jeers of agreement. In a bid to rescue events, the Guru timidly suggested that they could, perhaps, pass an hour by heading across the pasture to pick daisies with which to make leis for later.

Arms folded, the Buddha was unfazed. "You all know where there's a SuperMacs, Hungry Jacks and Big Macs if you want fast food," came the sure-footed return of serve. Tom Petty restored order when he strummed the opening chords of 'Freefalling' and everyone joined in the chorus.

Elsewhere, Philo had arrived down out of the clouds. He was a sight for sore eyes and caused pure bedlam after being egged on to strike up 'Dancing in the Moonlight'. The bass intro was enough to scramble everyone to their feet, hands in the air, hands in their hair, hands everywhere. The Buddha stole a glance and smile at Grażyna across the fire, as he and the flames swayed to the rhythm of Philo's perfectly plucked bassline. The smile on Philo's face. Everyone dancing in the moonlight. It was to be the last gathering at which the Buddha ever saw Philo.

More guests. The Professor and Felix. Buddha waved out a welcome and in the process slightly overdid it, as if to say that there wouldn't be any repeat of the Mexican standoff that happened the last time he encountered Felix on the banks of the Thames. The matter of life and death that had led to a heated exchange that evening was whether 'Once Upon A Time in the West' was the greatest movie ever made. That 'better' and 'best' stuff always bothered the Buddha. Relieved that peace had broken out, the Professor scanned the fireside for a fan with whom he could hopefully discuss that other matter of life and death – and even more important still: sport.

"Supper is served. Soul food for the weary souls," sounded the Buddha with a flourish and, with hunger on his side, no one had to be asked twice to be seated. Biker, Runner, Guru and Dodo served up the Mount Rath Moussaka as Buddha surveyed the gallery of faces flickering in and out of the night. Many were friends; others, he had never seen before. "Bon

Appetit," blessed the Buddha, to which echoed the reply "Smacznego" and, somewhere out of the dark, "Mark Killalea," to a mirthful murmurs.

With Grażyna's famous garlic and naan breads and green salad now doing the rounds, the circle was hushed in homage of this fine food. As the moussaka was mopped, praise punctuated the slow return of conversation:

"Super bomba."

"Delicious."

"Magnifico" (that was Biker taking the piss).

"Lekker," said another, nodding vigorously.

"As Brad Pitt might say, 'Bonjourno,'" gabbed Killer.

"Pyszne, pyszne," Rebecca and Gemma said, only to spark the Gura off into "Hare Krishna, Hare Krishna, Krishna, Krishna, Hare Rama, Hare Rame," which had Philo – and soon everyone – on to their feet, dancing in the moonlight like little children in circles, back and forth around the fire.

Zoom arrived just in time with Shergar, out of god-knows-where, promptly producing a tambourine, maracas and a button accordion, before giving it socks. Out of somewhere, a sax could be heard. More whistles and beaming smiles. The djembes joined in and drove it off the charts: Hare Krishna, Hare Krishna, Krishna Krishna, Hare, Hare, Hare Rama, Hare Rame, Rama Rama, Hare Hare.

Kite lanterns, fireflies, the stars, skinny bellies, potbellies and smelly bellies all dancing in the moonlight. Across the Gathering, it played out. Infectious. A soul for every star in that crazy night sky. Slightly different words, strange accents, yet all in tune, even if they were singing different songs.

The Buddha slipped away beneath an old oak, beckoning Dodo, the comforting rhythms ringing in their ears, dancers silhouetted. "You know, you can change that recipe to suit your own taste and use courgettes or potatoes instead of the aubergines. You can put in some celery or parsnip and some ground cumin, mixed in with the lentils, gives it a lovely flavour," the Buddha pontificated, rubbing his chin absent-mindedly and half-looking into the night. Dodo, however, had him copped on and his grimace and sideways glance said so.

"Okay, sorry for beating 'round the bush, it's not my form. Can you tell me again, Dodo, what it is they've been saying down in the Chai kitchen?" the Buddha asked, confessing his weakness for the gossip. Dodo sighed and took a deep breath, as he looked on at what seemed like the whole world dancing in the moonlight.

Next morning, Dodo still got a sense of sadness hanging over the Buddha. "You seem sad," he prompted.

"I am."

"You look worried too."

"I am."

"Surely no need to worry here, among friends."

"You misunderstand Dodo. It is my friends, not I, that I'm worried for."

And so the stage was set for a showdown between the Buddha and his detractors in the talking circle. The Buddha started off by appealing to what he knew was the clans' and tribes' great love of nature. He told them of how, in 1854, the Great White Chief in Washington made an offer for a large area of Indian land and promised peace and a 'reservation' for the Indian people. This was Chief Seattle's reply:

"How can you buy or sell the sky, the warmth of the land? The idea is strange to us. If we do not own the freshness of the air and the sparkle of the water, how can you buy them?

"Every part of this earth is sacred to my people. Every shining pine needle, every sandy shore, every mist in the dark woods, every clearing and humming insect is holy in the memory and experience of my people. The sap which courses through the trees carries the memories of the red man.

"The white man's dead forget the country of their birth when they go to walk among the stars. Our dead never forget this beautiful earth, for it is the mother of the red man. We are part of the earth and it is part of us. The perfumed flowers are our sisters; the deer, the horse, the great eagle, these are our brothers. The rocky crests, the horses in the meadows, the body heat of the pony, and man — all belong to the same family.

"So, when the Great Chief in Washington sends word that he wishes to buy our land, he asks much of us. The Great Chief sends word he will reserve us a place so that we can live comfortably to ourselves. He will be our father and we will be his children. So, we will consider your offer to buy our land. But it will not be easy. For this land is sacred to us. This shining water that moves in the streams and rivers is not just water but the blood of our ancestors. If we sell you land you must remember that it is sacred, and you must teach your children that it is sacred and that each ghostly reflection in the clear water of the lakes tells of events and memories in the life of my people. The water's murmur is the voice of my father's father.

"The rivers are our brothers, they quench our thirst. The rivers carry our canoes and feed our children. If we sell you our land, you must remember to teach your children, that the rivers are our brothers and yours, and you must henceforth give the rivers the kindness you would give any brother. We know that the white man does not understand our ways. One portion of land is the same to him as the next, for he is a stranger who comes in the night and takes from the land whatever he needs. The earth is not his brother, but his enemy, and when he has conquered it, he moves on. He leaves his father's grave behind, and he does not care. He kidnaps the earth from his children, and he does not care. His father's grave, and his children's birthright, are forgotten. He treats his mother, the earth, and his brother, the sky as things to be bought, plundered, sold like sheep or bright beads. His appetite will devour the earth and leave behind only a desert.

"I do not know. Our ways are different from your ways. The sight of your cities pains the eyes of the red man. But perhaps it is because the red man is a savage and does not understand. There is no quiet place in the white man's cities. No place to hear the unfurling of leaves in spring, or the rustle of an insect's wings. But perhaps it is because I am a savage and do not understand. The clatter only seems to insult the ears. And what is there to life if a man cannot hear the lonely cry of the whippoorwill or the arguments of the frogs around a pond at night? I am a red man and do not understand. The Indian prefers the soft sound of the wind darting over the face of a pond, and the smell of the wind itself, cleaned by a midday rain, or scented with the pinion pine.

"The air is precious to the red man, for all things share the same breath – the beast, the tree, the man, they all share the same breath. The white man does not seem to notice the air he breathes. Like a man dying for many days, he is numb to the stench. But if we sell you our land, you must remember that the air is precious to us, that the air shares its spirit with all the life it supports. The wind that gave our grandfather his first breath also receives his last sigh. And if we sell our land, you must keep it apart and sacred, as a place where even the white man can go to taste the wind that is sweetened by the meadow's flowers.

"So, we will consider your offer to buy our land. If we decide to accept, I will make one condition: The white man must treat the beasts of this land as his brothers. I am a savage and I do not understand any other way. I have seen a thousand rotting buffaloes on the prairie, left by the white man who shot them from a passing train. I am a savage and I do not understand how the smoking iron horse can be more important than the buffalo that we kill only to stay alive. What is a man without the beasts? If all the beasts were gone, man would die from a great loneliness of spirit. For whatever happens to the beasts, soon happens to man. All things are connected.

"You must teach your children that the ground beneath their feet is the ashes of your grandfathers. So that they will respect the land, tell your children that the earth is rich with the lives of our kin. Teach your children what we have taught our children, that the earth is our mother. Whatever befalls the earth befalls the sons of the earth. If men spit upon the ground, they spit upon themselves. This we know: The earth does not belong to man; man belongs to the earth. This we know.

"All things are connected, like the blood which unites one family. All things are connected. Whatever befalls the earth befalls the sons of the earth. Man did not weave the web of life; he is merely a strand in it. Whatever he does to the web, he does to himself. Even the white man, whose God walks and talks with him as friend to friend, cannot be exempt for the common destiny. We may be brothers after all. We shall see. One thing we know, which the white man may one day discover – our God is the same God.

"You may think that you know Him as you wish to own our land; but you cannot. He is the God of man, and his compassion is equal for the red man and the white. This earth is precious to Him, and to harm the earth is to heap contempt on its Creator.

"The whites too shall pass, perhaps sooner than all other tribes. Contaminate your bed, and you will one night suffocate in your own waste.

But in your perishing you will shine brightly, fired by the strength of the God who brought you to this land and for some special purpose gave you dominion over this land and over the red man.

"That destiny is a mystery to us, for we do not understand when the buffalo are all slaughtered, the wild horses are tamed, the secret corners of the forest heavy with the scent of many men, and the view of the ripe hills blotted by talking wires.

"Where is the thicket? Gone. Where is the eagle? Gone. The end of living and the beginning of survival."

"More stories, more parables from your travels; you have one for everyone in the audience, no doubt," taunted Ballinspittle the Barapasaurus, unmoved by the Buddha's speech.

"Do you think we came down in the last shower?" prodded Knock the Kentrosaurus, reminding the gathering that one of the Buddha's previous stories was that of sunflowers that grew up to the sky. Now he wanted them to take seriously his folklore of pending doom.

"As for the sunflowers, I have seen them and grown them myself, like 'Jack and the Beanstalks', with stems as thick as tree stumps, in Cremorgan," the Buddha uttered, getting sidetracked unnecessarily.

"Yes, and those who have climbed them – not yourself of course – have burned in the flames of the sun like Icarus," Ballinspittle said, drawing a barrage of derision.

"Not necessarily. There are those who have climbed for the stars, like Ever Ramirez, who have not returned. Perhaps they have not yet reached the top or, once they did, liked it so much that they decided to stay there in the warmth of the sun," argued the Buddha, getting nowhere.

"This is not the Stone Age. We are not stupid numbskulls and yet you persist with your talk of some far-fetched holocaust for the want of water. It's absurd," bickered Grallagh the Gargoyleosaurus, finding some favour with the throng, which had now swelled the talking circle.

"You are right: you are not stupid – you simply do not listen. I don't speak of the Stone Age but of the Carn Age, where all they eat is meat and where they are consumed by consuming," the Buddha railed, to gasps of horror around the circle.

"They even have designer dogs," he continued.

"You mean dogs that look like handbags?" asked Ballyhooly, trying to give the Buddha the benefit of the doubt.

"No, that's not what I mean, but yes, that too. But they are breeding dogs that cannot breathe any longer, as their snouts are so small. In-breeding for Labradoodles – Labradors crossed with Poodles that will not shed hair; Spoodles – spaniels that can nearly talk to you, and Cavoodles – Cavaliers crossed with Poodles, who really think they're something and would never dream of lying up on a couch. And Noodles..."

"What do they breed them for?" came a question from the crowd.

"To eat! Just like they eat everything else and Cock-a-Do-a-Doodles and I'm not even going to go there in front of the children," contended the Buddha.

"This is pure ridiculous," charged Knock, having heard enough already. "No people who cared for their children one whit would behave this way."

"I am almost done and you leave me no choice but to confront you with what may be an inconvenient truth," warned the Buddha, who had hoped to avoid any histrionics. "There are days ahead where there is nothing else only plague and pestilence, floods, convulsions and landslides. Tsunamis of torment that destroy all in their path, leaving no trace, the tragedy so big that the people stop counting the dead in their desperate haste to forget what has happened. In one bout of the Spanish flu alone, forty million died and as many since of starvation. There is a time on earth when there are no living traces of the Dinosaur Clans or Rainbow Tribes," the Buddha announced, to unbridled uproar and a venomous chorus of charges against him.

On cue, Dodo stepped forward and, with the Buddha's walking pole, etched out in the soil at the centre of the circle the word 'Xtinct'.

In this terrible moment, the Buddha himself had an epiphany and shockingly realised that Dodo could neither read nor write. But while Dodo would learn, the Buddha also realised that there were those who would never learn.

CHAPTER X

If it walks like a duck…

'I beg your pardon,
I never promised you a rose garden
Along with the sunshine,
There's gotta be a little rain sometime.'

"Respect Dong," said Buddha as he greeted the King, almost falling over himself thanks to Tub Tusz getting in under his feet. The Dong grimaced and grunted out his usual welcome. "How was your time with your friends? Surfers aren't they? Then there's the witches and, of course, the Dinosaur Clans, at your secret gathering in Ballyhuppahaun." The Dong's spies had been busy. "I see, Buddha, that after all I've done for you and yours, you stumble in here, one arm longer than the other, with not a carrot of gold or even an ounce of gratitude."

As he opened his mouth to respond, the Buddha was momentarily startled by a loud explosion. One of the twelve great fountains of the Dongdom had erupted, spewing a waterfall into the sky. The King loved the shock and awe it created. It was truly spectacular. The exploding one was called Mount Vesuvius, as all twelve fountains were named after the great volcanoes of the world. They were a constant source of reassurance to the King's loyal subjects that they lived in a land of plenty. Water was the fountain of life and, each year, they would journey for miles to see the cascades for themselves, and maybe even catch a glimpse of the King. The fountains were so vast that each could be viewed from the balcony of the great hall, off the Dong's quarters. There was Mount Etna, Mount Fuji, Pinatuba, Mount Unzen, Avachinsky, Kilauea, Ruapehu, Akutan, Cerro Negro, Stromboli, Katla and, of course, Vesuvius.

"When all twelve rain down simultaneously and at the same time it is but a small measure of the greatness and bounty of the King and the Dongdom. He is showering us with plenty and abundance," spoke The Senator, who was both fond of waxing lyrical and the Dong's favourite politician. Yes, The Senator truly had a way with words and styled himself as a persecuted saint and scholar. He quoted liberally from the classics and stayed on side with the Druids as he lauded the carbolic influence of the Church on the plebs.

Well, if it took butter to buttress his relationship with the Dong then so be it, thought Buddha. He would butter them up and choke them on honey. Looking out across the panorama offered by the massive windows, framing mown lawns and manicured gardens, the Buddha could not help but notice too the tuneful choruses chirped by the nightingales, linnets and blackbirds that lined the branches. In a jolt of déjà vu – or was it a daydream or dreamtime – the Buddha was sure that he had seen that exact sight and heard those very sounds before.

Still watching, the Buddha was relieved to see the fountains shooting off in sequence and, during that event, became almost mesmerised. If the Dongdom could boast such wealth and affluence of resources and grandour, perhaps all was well. Maybe his fears and his foreboding were unfounded. Were there some prospects, then, of a modus vivendi with His Majesty?

"The gift of giving is so much greater than the getting. It is ordained and the lot of mere mortals to be on the receiving end, Mighty Dong," the Buddha contended. Uncertain as to the depth of the Buddha's sincerity, the Dong, who was now sitting on his throne, said, "Explain". Leaning onto his rainstick and buying some time, the Buddha thought that he should explain indeed – explain as one would to a child.

"First, let me introduce my travelling companions: Bengal the Hare, The Skibbereen Eagle and, somewhere or other, Tup Tusz the turtle." Tup Tusz had disappeared again. Buddha had urged Dodo and the others to stay behind and enjoy their time in Ballyhuppahaun. He had brought the Skibbereen Eagle to keep an eye on things, after they had linked up on the roadtrip in West Cork. Bengal, a longtime friend, had offered to tag along, while Tup Tusz had insisted. Tup Tusz had only awoken on the last night of the surf trip, in the middle of the didge party, at the height of the Kangaroo Moon. No one ever knew if he was dead or alive until he came out of his shell. He had been full of beans ever since.

Buddha had completely forgotten about Yorn, his other companion, until the hob-tailed skink had let out a groan and lashed his elastic-like long blue tongue around a bluebottle that wouldn't be making a nuisance of itself anymore. For the first time, it had occurred to the Buddha that this might explain the blue tongue. Everyday is a school day, he reminded himself with a smile.

"Something amusing that you'd like to share with us?" quizzed the Dong, who was finding the Buddha's dallying tiresome, even though His Majesty was being massaged and swanned over by a swarm of servants. One such servant was busy filing his toes, while another plucked his eyebrows. Each hair that was tweezered was followed by a sneeze from the King. It wasn't until the Dong had ordered the Buddha to get on with it that it was certain the King was sitting there on the throne at all, such was the level of activity. He was now drinking his favourite brew from a tankard.

The Buddha, about to launch into his treatise on the wealth of giving, noticed that the choir of birds on the branches had stopped singing and appeared to be standing still in the evening sun.

"It is fine; don't worry in the slightest. The little creatures have sung their happy little hearts out for the King. They will be removed and replaced overnight by the royal ornithologists, so that the lyric can refrain once more at first light in a dawn chorus for the Dong," flapped the Senator, who was in danger of losing sight of daylight himself if he went any further for the Dongdom, clearly inebriated by the exuberance of his own verbosity.

Yorn, oblivious, lamped another bluebottle. Tup Tusz then appeared from beneath the Buddha, stuck his head out and stared up quizzically, trying to make eye contact. He urged the Buddha to press on with his parable, or he too would be sticking his neck out too far. The Buddha relinquished and narrated his tale:

"While Seisetsu was the master of Engaku in Kamakura he required larger quarters, since those in which he was teaching were overcrowded. Umezu Seibei, a merchant of Edo, decided to donate five hundred pieces of gold – called ryo – toward the construction of a more commodious school. This money he brought to the teacher, who said, 'Alright, I will take it.'

"Umezu gave Seisetsu the sack of gold, but he was dissatisfied with the attitude of the teacher. One might live a whole year on three ryo, and the merchant had not even been thanked for five hundred. 'In that sack are five hundred ryo,' hinted Umezu. 'You told me that before,' Seisetsu replied.

'Even if I am a wealthy merchant, five hundred ryo is a lot of money,' said Umezu. 'Do you want me to thank you for it?' asked Seisetsu. 'You ought to,' Umezu answered. 'Why should I?' inquired Seisetsu, adding, 'The giver should be thankful.'"

"So, we are supposed to be grateful to you?" fumed the Dong, after hearing the tale. This sanctimonious bastard would try the patience of any man, he thought, even a great leader like himself.

"Perhaps we missed the moral of the story," The Senator hurriedly interjected, not wanting to see this prophet's head on a plate – in his presence at least. "This Zen business all sounds as cryptic and complex as our beloved Joyce and Beckett. Perhaps you can elaborate and explain," he added. The Senator knew full well that the King was minded to having the Buddha and his menagerie of mates for breakfast – in a manner of speaking, of course – before having them hanged, drawn and quartered in traditional style, and finally impaled on the City gates as an example to all. But for the love and honour of god, the Dong and the Kingdom, how on earth was he supposed to go to the Senate and honestly deny all knowledge of such events if they were to (to use the language of the hoi polloi) kick off now, in his very presence.

Not surprisingly, however, there was about as much chance now of the Yorn holding his tongue as the Buddha. "May I request a cup of tea?" the Buddha asked politely, ignoring the wrath festering in the room.

"Pardon me and our outrageously bad manners," replied the Senator, while fussily clapping his hands for service.

"No bother; a cup of tea in the hand is fine," assured the Buddha, who, not for the first time, had not been offered a morsel amid the lavish settings.

"Very lovely, very lovely," Buddha noted with a sigh, realising that he had spent too much time on the road with Lava Lava as the words left his lips and he sipped on the tea. Tup Tusz looked on, wide-eyed and anxious now, not knowing what to expect of the Buddha and wishing he could go back to sleep again.

The Dong had had enough of the Buddha's insolence and would press on now with his home advantage.

"What, Buddha, would make a man truly wealthy, healthy and happy?" The Dong had thought to steer the Buddha in the direction of food, water and plenty for all, in order to lasso him with a noose of his own making.

Not for the first time though, the Buddha would rely on the sure-footed teaching of the masters.

"A rich man asked Sengai the monk to write something for the continued prosperity of his family so that it might be treasured from generation to generation. Sengai obtained a large sheet of paper and wrote: 'Father dies, son dies, grandson dies.'

"The rich man became angry. 'I asked you to write something for the happiness of my family! Why do you make such a joke as this?' Sengai explained that no joke or offence was intended. 'If before you yourself die your son should die, this would grieve you greatly. If your grandson should pass away before your son, both of you would be broken-hearted. If your family, generation after generation, passes away in the order I have named, it will be the natural course of life. I call this real prosperity.'"

The Dong left without another word but he got the message. There would be no pact with the Buddha and his kind. Furthermore, he was not even sure if this latest little story did not contain a veiled threat to his unborn son and heir. He now would have to teach this Buddha a lesson he would never forget.

Chapter XI

The Paddy Fields

'Inch by inch, row by row,
Gonna make this garden grow,
Gonna mulch it deep and low,
Gonna make it fertile ground.'

"When you eat, eat," the Buddha admonished Dodo but tempered the harshness of his instruction with a smile, as all he seemed to be doing these past few days was giving out to Dodo and that was not his intention in the scheme of things at all. So much had he wanted this time to be special that he himself was now forcing and spoiling things in the process. It was time to listen to his own lessons.

Still, Buddha wanted Dodo to stop tappin', pokin' and fidgetin', to relax and enjoy the view and the food. He had a better chance of Dodo heeding him if he did a little less restless pacing from one foot to the other, like a tethered, tormented elephant who was about to turn turk.

"Spuds go with almost everything; they're great like that and tasty out too with a knob of butter and a pinch of salt. They're pure mighty mashed with scallions and you know how popular my famous fried potatoes are. I'll let you in on the secret of how to do them properly," Buddha said.

Dodo's face dropped in dismay at the Buddha's advice and his latest, bewildering, evasiveness. After months of ducking, diving, and dodging, the Buddha had finally promised to tell Dodo about the birds and bees, once they had gotten back from the road trip and before he set off again on his travels. That was prior to being beckoned again by the Dong though. That summons seemed to knock the Buddha out of his stride and make him more distant than he was on any of his far-flung journeys. Nevertheless, Dodo had often heard whispers about the birds and the bees and was sick of all this cogar mogar.

"Advice is not always what it's cracked up to be," reasoned the Buddha, trying to change the subject again. "Christy Ring had the right idea and was shocking slow to be dishing out advice. When he eventually did, as I told you before..."

"I know, I know. 'Keep your eye on the ball, even if the ref have it'," Dodo finished off the Buddha's sentence with exaggerated enthusiasm.

"You'd do well to keep that in mind," persisted the Buddha, while attempting to ignore the strains of derision in Dodo's tone.

"Advice is often misunderstood, misheard, misinterpreted or just plain mischief, and what is it only someone telling you how to avoid the mistakes they have already made. You keep your eye on the ball and you won't go too far wrong," Buddha advised.

"I am keeping one eye on the birds-and-the-bees ball and the other one on you," rounded Dodo, laying down a marker in a manner that the Buddha quite admired.

"Fair enough," shrugged the Buddha. "The question of the birds and the bees is no trifling matter but the very essence of life itself. It is not something to be flippant or flap about, but it's to be taken slowly and skillfully, so we will deal with the birds and the bees this evening after supper. Once you know, there will never again be any turning back for you to the age of innocence. Now, what do you think of my spuds?"

Ever since Black '47, the Buddha had a fixation with spuds. He'd seldom talk about it. The scars ran deeper than any left by the swords or switchblades he had encountered. Unlike all his other experiences, the Buddha refused to speak about those deadly, diseased days on the Emerald Isle. "'Give a man a fish and you feed him for a day; teach a man to fish and you feed him forever.' I once heard you say on a surf trip that there are plenty of fish in the sea," Dodo had said to Buddha the previous evening, offering what he thought was a well-intentioned and helpful suggestion. A frowning glance from the Buddha, however, had stopped that train of thought in its tracks. "So many fields, so many farmers and so little food; is that fishy enough for you?" the Buddha had retorted, cutting the socks from underneath Dodo but regretting it the moment the words left his lips.

"The most important thing in the world is to know how to sow a seed and save some water," the Buddha now insisted, as proud as punch that he had finally gotten to show off what he affectionately called the Paddy Fields in Borraderra to Dodo.

As far as the eye could see, spuds. All sorts of spuds. This is where the Buddha had learned the fine art of vegetable farming from his father. How to beat the carrot fly, who could sniff out the strong scent of a freshly pulled carrot for miles. Or how to get the better not only of the slugs and caterpillars, who wouldn't leave you with a head of cabbage or cauliflower, but also, as his father would call them, "those pesky wabbits", who wouldn't settle for anything other than the sweetest lettuce and radish leaves.

In Ballyhuppahaun, the Buddha would tend to his awesome array of veggies, ranging from asparagus and aubergines to zucchinis, whereas here in Borraderra, where he had toiled and learned his craft, it was the preserve of the humble potato, the Paddy Fields. Here, he had barrowed dung, dug drills and made beds. It was here that he first learned the delight and awe of how a speck of seed – often a mere fleck of dust – could, in weeks, germinate and grow into a delicious herb or veg. It still didn't seem possible to him that you could drop a tiny black dot into the soil, simply add water, sit back and let nature do the rest, perhaps giving her a little dig out with the pests, of course. All the more reason why a fury welled up in him when he thought of all those fields, all those farmers and yet so much famine. Where was the sense, rhyme or reason to that blight on all our souls, he would despairingly ask himself.

"Famine," Buddha fumed, "a blight on all our souls." Rice is good, but spuds are great, he regularly stated, happy to propagate the pleasure of the potato at every opportunity. He would energetically propagate the actual potato crop too, as if he was setting out to feed the planet. "Plough those fields," was an order he would drill into anyone who'd listen, as he spread seed potatoes from Borraderra to Beijing and back to Ballyhuppahaun via Babylon.

Catriona, Charlotte, Desiree, Orla, Celine and Nicola; the Buddha loved them all and would sing their praises and care for them daily. However, the Rooster was his top of the pops. A firm favourite it was, the old Rooster in its red skin. "Balls of flour, balls of flour," he would pronounce, as if from a pulpit. He would also relish a roasted Golden Wonder and seldom pass a Kerr's Pink, or Sharpe's Express for early success.

"So many spuds, and, like myself, best taken with a pinch of salt," he joked as he emerged from his recollections, before adding in foreboding fashion, "A new famine stalks the land. This time the spuds won't fail us Dodo – we will fail ourselves." After a few moments of uneasy silence,

Buddha opted to lighten the mood: "So, after supper, Dodo, the birds and the bees. The birds and the bees and your time has come."

By now anxious with anticipation, Dodo had been slicing spuds, onions and garlic in preparation for their meal and, afterwards, their long-awaited chat. The aroma of Buddha's freshly baked bread wafted across the sacred well after being taken from the kiln, another of his ingenious devices. Butter not long from the churn chilled in the babbling brook, out of the gaze of the evening sun. Supper was shaping up.

In Borraderra the chip butty was king. The Buddha had collected a half-dozen eggs from a girl on the Curragh, in gratitude for a sup of water he had spared. He hadn't stopped going on since about her foxy locks of hair, and she making her way from Boolavogue to the Bog of Allen. "The birds and the bees indeed," the Buddha caught himself muttering as he sneaked a look out from under his eyebrows to see if Dodo had copped. Instead, he saw Dodo crying and rubbing his face, with the backs of his hands buried to the wrists in his eye sockets; squirming tearfully, thanks to the stinging Bedfordshire Champions, as much preferred by the Buddha for their long storing as for their heavy cropping here (although he only grew a small patch) in the beds of Borraderra, Skirteen and Cow Pasture.

The Buddha, if he was let, would talk about nothing else except vegetables, rambling on about the old days and how things were so much better back then. People knew how to grow things and everyone got to grow up in their own time, he would say nostalgically. He remembered one year when the cabbage had been shredded by the caterpillars, before they had wised up to the benefits of having a couple of hedgehogs about. A sneak attack, out of the morning sun, by those Stuka dive-bombers of carrot flies had riddled that season's crop to shreds. By the time the slugs and rabbits had had their fill there was nothing left but brussels sprouts and beetroot. All that year, he recalled with a grimace, it was brussels sprouts, brown bread and beetroot soup. Frogspawn-tasting tapioca for afters.

"Eat up those greens, they're good for ye," his mother would lilt, singing the praises of sprouts in season. That year, it seemed as if they were in season for twelve months. When his uncle Mick would visit, his mother would deliberately serve up beetroot soup to a recipe called barszcz, which she had picked up on her extensive travels throughout Europe. She knew his stomach heaved at the mere mention of the word 'beetroot', let alone actually looking into a bowl of the blood red broth. Had it in for him somehow and all you'd ever hear, out across the half-door as he headed down the boreen, was, "He thought he'd never get her."

"Did you ever have a beetroot sandwich, Dodo? That's all meself and the Scholar Connolly had in Carnsore in '78, and we trying to keep the nukes out," Dodo mimed the sentence, as the Buddha was like a long-playing record when he started on about 'back in the day'.

On went the Buddha: "Very few pleasures to compare to those of a voluptuous vegetable bed. What a sight. Like the first twinkle in the eye of a white cauliflower floret, just nuzzling out; the tempting jet pupil of a blackcurrant; the juice of a ripe tomato running down your chin; the inviting pink-red radish, pouting and pursed against the soil; brushing against brazen basil and dill, a delirious perfume; the tingling sensation on your tongue of a chopped chilli; spicy rocket ready to explode; luscious lettuce with beads of rain dripping down its veins; turnips round and firm..."

"Will you cut it out, you and your vegetables!" Dodo finally bawled. "Talk about garlic or something."

"Grand mouth ye have for garlic. It's far from garlic you were reared," the Buddha teased, mimicking a chastising he had often gotten from his own granny. "I'll bake you a bread pudding for dessert after supper so," the Buddha cajoled, by way of a peace offering to the now sulking Dodo. He had bread left over this two days and he'd go by the recipe of that magician in the kitchen from Mount Rath, second only to the ones his mother made, with fresh custard too. As she never tired of saying, "Waste not, want not".

Bread and butter pudding was always in season and it was Dodo's favourite dish by far. The Buddha had the bread, butter, eggs and 'curns', and he was certain to run Dodo down to Spain's parlour in Old Grange for fresh milk. "The loveliest, creamiest milk this side of Outer Mongolia," the Buddha would sometimes brag about the parlour, setting himself up to deliver a later scolding when Dodo would inevitably slouch back, tardy by hours, after chasing frogs across the soggy fields. Buddha would ask thunderously, "Where did ye go for the milk – Outer Mongolia, was it?"

Bread pudding, the birds and the bees; Dodo was beside himself with this double treat. Having the Buddha rave on about the medicinal powers of garlic was a small price to pay. "Cure your heart and cleanse your soul; no ould wives' tales," he would lecture, getting carried away.

"Have you a cure for a broken heart?" Shagmire had asked the Buddha once, cornering him and he full to the gills. "Rub garlic on it. Garlic cures everything," was the swift response. That was the end of another great romance. Indeed, there were times when the Buddha could well have come back as a garlic clove, as its aroma wafted from every pore in his hide. He reeked of it. He'd put it in bread and butter pudding if you let him.

The Buddha, without doubt, held garlic in high esteem. It was in Cremorgan, at the back of the Round Tower, where he grew a crop to rival any French or Spanish flavours you fancied, and he wouldn't entertain talk of Chinese garlic at all, at all. "Why would you go to China for garlic when you can grow it here in Cremorgan?" he'd challenge. Every year, he'd gently break open the bulbs and plant out each clove with painstaking care in a patch prepared beside the orchard of apple, plums and pears. He'd have it in by November to beat the first frosts, as the garlic snuggled down for the winter, licking lips at the likelihood of icy morns.

"Garlic's not high maintenance, I tell ye. All you have to do with it is wait," Buddha frequently boasted, complimenting himself on his patience and not just the prowess of the all-curing garlic – which, you'd swear sometimes, he had invented, given the way he went on. "If I had a child, I'd call it Garlic. Whether it was a boy or a girl, I'd call it Garlic," he blackguarded Dodo. "It's every bit as good as some of those new-fangled names you hear about." He was still failing to draw Dodo however, who wasn't going to spoil this evening. Engrossed, the pair had scarcely noticed the sun shower, a sturdy rainbow across the fields in its aftermath, the sun setting and seesawing with the emerging moon.

Wait until the following August he would, when all the stems turned an autumn golden yellow. Only then would the Buddha fork out his beloved garlic's newest crop, one of his favourite days of the year.

At the edge of the Paddy Fields in Borraderra ran a stream so small that it was not even deserving of a name. It was here that the Buddha and Dodo had tucked in for the evening, the fire lit and stars happy out, playing hide-and-seek, as if the fairy lights slung through the canopy of the willow trees had been chosen as their thrones. Now, polishing off the last of the pudding with a cup of tea from the fresh well water, the Buddha, in his contentment, was inclined to ponder pervasively on the postprandial dip.

"Grossly misunderstood," he uttered abruptly, leaving his assessment hanging in the air.

"What, the birds and the bees?" Dodo sat up to attention.

"No; have you nothing else on the brain, only the birds and the bees?" The Buddha joshed.

"You're not on about garlic again, surely?" Dodo feared another one of Buddha's delaying tactics or, worse again, another deferral of his moment of truth. That would be a pure disaster altogether.

"No, leave the garlic out of it. Willows, weeping willows and pussy willows – grossly misunderstood. Mistaken for being sad and weak, when nothing could be further from the truth. Like so many things, when you think about it, just like the birds and the bees, Dodo – grossly misunderstood."

He had Dodo's undivided attention. What harm was there in a little rambling from the Buddha, thought Dodo, when there was so much at stake.

"The birds and the bees, Dodo, is a matter of life and death," the Buddha relayed in hushed tones, as if the cabbages and cauliflowers in the next field had ears. Well into the night, he proceeded to explain the mystery and wonder of the birds and the bees to Dodo.

"How many times have you seen Vanessa this summer?" The Buddha asked, already in charge of the answer.

"Once, I guess."

"You guess right, Dodo. Vanessa, the Painted Lady. Or, more correctly, Vanessa Cardui, the Latin name of this beauty," Buddha divulged. As if he did not have enough on his plate, the Buddha had most recently roped Dodo into his latest exploit, lepidopterology, the study of moths and butterflies.

"So, to put it another way Dodo, in ten summers' time, ten Painted Ladies later and that's the end of bees. The end of bees forever."

Dodo was stunned. His world shattered. This is not at all what he had expected of the birds and the bees. Still, it now seemed perfectly clear to him why everyone should speak of such a tragedy in whispers. Bees – extinct? No wonder his father had never spoken to him about this. It was hard to take in, impossible to understand. At least the Buddha had held his nerve and got through imparting the news to Dodo as best he could. Dodo was shaken from his daze by the sound of Buddha's voice.

"The bees, it seems, have had enough, overworked and underrated. Infected by a terrible sadness, they are dying in their droves; hive after hive never found alive or never found at all, but no one really knows how or why. It is one of the great mysteries of the world. Tens of billions of bees have lost their buzz and without them, there'll be no more flowers, fruit, shrubs and trees; no more birds and no more bees. All the King's men are working on it day and night but so far all they've come up with is Humpty Dumpty – one big duck egg." The Buddha saw no point in pulling his punches at this stage.

Dodo was devastated. Tears welling up in his eyes, he couldn't believe his ears. "Bees extinct? What are we going to do? You said that we all need honey at least once a week to keep us sweet and healthy. We can't survive without it, you said," Dodo moaned, in a terrible state.

"What's this 'we' business, paleface?" Buddha tried to ease the tension. "It's time to tell a new story, one that has not yet been written. Some say the birds might have the answer as to why the bees are so sad, but to understand them you have to be for the birds. No such person, a birdman with a bird's eye view, has yet revealed himself. Our only hope may be with a real birdbrain; someone who can understand the constant chatter of the winged, warbling and waddling ones." Having said this, the Buddha quietly slipped around the back of the tree, as nature called.

"No more bees; it's hard to believe." Dodo was half hoping that Buddha would reappear armed with some revelation, but what he heard as the Buddha emerged from behind the weeping willow was not what he was praying for.

"Lynch from Leix, near The Rock of Dunamaise, may be the last beekeeper. No more honey, no more honeysuckle, no more honeymoons. With bees gone, can us human beings be far behind?"

Dodo slumped, speechless. He had never been as sad before as he was now, at the Paddy Fields in Borraderra.

CHAPTER XII

The Battle of the Burren

'Funny how fallin' feels like flyin',
For a little while.'

There are no accounts of the Battle of the Burren to be found in the Book of Invasions, the Book of Kells, The Táin, The Annals of the Four Masters, or any of the other ancient Celtic scripts. While the Dong was a past master in the black art of re-writing history, he did not have to try too hard on this occasion to twist the arms of the paparazzi. He did not opt for a 'Year Zero', 'Ground Zero' or a 'New Dawn', as his senators and special advisors had proposed. The slogan, 'The Heroes of Ground Zero', had been bandied about, but the Dong thought better of having any more heroes about the place, either dead or alive. 'New Dawn' had a certain cultured, renaissance ring to it, but the Dong was never much of a morning person. In the end, he went with his own favourite suggestion, a 'New Age'.

The Dong and his allies started preparing for the aftermath of their certain victory in battle long before the first blow was ever struck. Once they had contrived just cause, justice had to be served and justification with the masses was secured. To copper-fasten his cause, the Dong employed emissaries and musicians, from opposite ends of the scale, as it were. To do his dirty work on the ground and to spread the gospel gossip of gluttony and gloating (while so many went without) and of witchery and debauchery (in a land of such decorum), the Dong had only to host a reception in his country residence for the Loodheramauns.

The Loodheramauns were from Lilliput, first cousins of the Amoeba who hailed from the same land. Their forefathers were famous for landing the right side up, no matter what the circumstances. The Amoeba were the silent types, while the Loodheramauns were the yappers in the family. Once taken into the King's confidence they could be relied on to go to the four corners and dish the dirt. The Loodheramauns were liable to say anything – a tendency the King counted on.

Music is the opium of the masses. This, the King counted on too, but musicians themselves were a different kettle of fish. If you could stuff the

Loodheramauns before having them for breakfast, you'd have to casserole musicians over a slow heat. They were, after all, artistes. Once the superstar Nobo agreed to headline the gig Dong had planned, the stage was set for a massive showcase, greater than any show of force the Dong could have dreamed of by simply parading his legions of warriors through the streets of the Eternal City, and then on tour through the White Cities of Babylon.

Nobo was anxious to speak to the people of the need to save water, indeed, save the world. He insisted upon this when he met the Dong, who kindly acquiesced to all Nobo's demands. "What mere mortal would dare stand in the path of such a noble mission?" he asked rhetorically, slapping Nobo on the back. "If only there were more like you that I could help in my own small way," the Dong continued, fulsomely praising the man he called the greatest living rock star ("Nay, the greatest of all time; a living legend"). "We will not stand idly by," Dong declared. "We will stand together on the world stage and fight side by side to save the world from self-destruction."

The wheels were in motion and it was music to the Dong's ears that the concert would go ahead on the World Stage, seven months hence – that being Valentine's Day in the Phoenix Park. The park itself, a fitting memorial to how the Dongdom had previously risen from the ashes, snatched victory from the jaws of defeat and defied the doomsayers. Zako was about his work in the Tatras, while the Dong's allies were already moving en masse on the seven seas. The bothersome Buddha, in the meantime, had been invited as a special guest to the Valentine's Day concert. What could possibly go wrong?

No one could resist such a line-up. Nobo, headlining, would be joined on the World Stage by another star attraction, Bobo, along with a supporting line-up of Thing, Up with People and the most recent winners of the universally popular X-Factor, The Easy Singles. To give the event a local flavour, the bill would be completed by The Seánies, who were thrilled that they would be the opening act on the day. Tickets would be free but in a sense priceless to the thousands upon thousands who would get their hands on them. The tickets were to be distributed, confetti-like, from the top of the Towers of Power. Everyone would want to be there, as there would never be a concert like this again. There was certain to be casualties in the stampede to secure access.

"Preparing the public for war is tougher than the fighting itself. Once we've won, it's vital that the people feel good about themselves, their sacrifice and the loved ones they have lost. No point in winning the war and losing the people, I always say," the Dong once confided to his close coterie of generals and financiers, as they oiled their war machine.

The seemingly endless rounds of wining and dining his backers, however, greatly tired the Dong. He had no time for these mealy-mouthed, milk and water types, and although he was no diplomat, he knew he had to truck with them. Then there was the media – or 'the meeja', as his favourite, wig-wearing Senator had sarcastically dubbed them – the gentlemen of the fourth estate. (The hacks for their part returned the affection by dubbing him The Rug). At least they both provided some mirth for His Majesty. "The paparazzi will do as they've always done," the Dong boasted, to the snickering of the elite from Les Congestez one evening on the balcony to his beloved gardens. "They will do what they're told."

When it came to war-speak, the Dong was in his element. Rousing talk came thick and fast from him: "In wars such as this, which is forced upon us, a war not to save ourselves but to save the world, we cannot take prisoners, lest we fall prisoner ourselves, delivered by enemy hands into the fickle court of public opinion. All is not fair in love, but in war. Moreover, if truth is the first casualty of war, is that not a fair price to pay to spare the lives of our people? A few fibs, such a foible, with so much at stake? A little white lie is sometimes best, lest the pale faces of our sons are left staring up at us from slabs down in the morgue. Better to feed a few lies to the masses than not to feed them at all." It was during times like this that the Dong was at his persuasive best. His chest puffed, his war chest swelled. He would blow the house down.

Next for the hallowed halls of the inner sanctum were 'the meeja'. They too would be fed. Stuffed with mead and served up merriment, they would get high on the hog and the honey. Embedded. Joined at the hip with high society. Gotcha! The hacks rubbed shoulders with the bankers, as one group shuffled in and the other shuttled out. A whispered request issued from the corner of a mouth to a source, asking for some insight. "He said he wants to feed the world and all is fair in love and war. He also said that never before had so many owed so much to so few," the source whispered back.

"Owed to who? The banks?"

"No – the press, you idiot. The people's press. I've got to go; don't let me down now."

In no time, wine flowed and the singsongs followed. The influential meeja were certainly under the influence now, as the Dong and his special advisors mingled with them. Ballads and bombast bombarded the night, with yarns ricocheting round the room. All very fine, until someone lost an eye.

"Whatever you say, say nothing
  When you talk about you know what
  For if you know who could hear you
  You know what you'd get
  For they'd take you off to you know where
  For you wouldn't know how long
  So for you know who's sake
  Don't let anyone hear you singing this song.
  And you all know what I'm speaking of
  When I mention you know what
  And I think it's very dangerous to even mention that
  For the other ones are always near
  Although you may not see
  And if anyone asks who told you that
  Please don't mention me.
  "And you all know who I'm speaking of
  When I mention you know who
  And if you know who could hear me
  You know what he'd do
  So if you don't see me around
  You'll know why I'm away
  And if anyone asks you where I've gone
  Here's what you must say.
  Well that's enough about so and so
  Not to mention such and such
  I think I'll end my song now
  Sure I've already said too much..."

Seldom, if ever, had the words of a ballad rang so true, even before the song was sung. The hack from the north was bundled out and never seen again. There lingered for a few days conflicting reports of his whereabouts and what exactly happened. Some said he hid and hung his head in shame, embarrassed by the shenanigans; others that he had even gone so far as to take his own life – something which the Dong himself had once advised all idle naysayers should do.

Still others contended that he was met with a malavogue and hung out to dry. In any event, he was never seen again. The song, which had been a favourite in the backstreet haunts of the hoi polloi, as long as the sands of time and ale had flowed, was never heard again.

There is no account of the Battle of the Burren in the Book of Invasions, the Book of Cells, the Táin or any other ancient scripts but as sure as you are sitting there, and as sure (for now at least) as night follows day, the battle took place in Clare. Signs of it still scar the landscape. Tales of it persist, never put to pen by scholars or scribes but passed on to generations, ó ghlúin go glúin. It is only ever faintly spoken of, with one eye on the latch, the other looking over the shoulder; the legend kept alive. The greatest story never told and never written of till now.

The Battle of the Burren was a bloodbath from start to finish. Neither side took any prisoners – other than those tortured and tormented until the last drop of use was wrung from their broken bodies and shattered spirits. The battle was waged and raged for one thousand days without let-up. The tactics were crude and cruel; the strategy, 'win at all cost'. The forces ranged against each other were fighting for the very survival of their race. A race against time. A race against extinction. In truth, the Battle of the Burren was more a holocaust than a war.

Backed into a corner, faced with the choice of fight or flight, the Rainbow Nations ended up doing both, with equal disarray and devastation. Had wiser counsel prevailed, and had they listened to the Buddha, there might have been less lives lost. However, lost tribes were not an option some could bear and so they instead bore the brunt of the brutality of war, as their families and friends fled in fear, forming frantic hopes of some escape.

The brutality and butchery that followed is so beyond words that it defies description. Your worst horrors pale, your numbing nightmares are nothing compared to the savage slaughter. Way worse than anything you have ever seen, heard of or imagined. A holocaust on a hill overlooking the Atlantic, at the Cliffs of Moher – a place then thought by all nations to be the ends of the earth. The Battle of the Burren would prove to be the end of the world as we know it.

In the build-up to the battle, everything had gone exactly to plan for the Dong. With lots of Big Brother Brew on tap, the crowds went rapturous in the Phoenix Park at the Valentine's Day Concert. "The mob loved it," the Dong boasted afterwards, as he told the Druids, who could only attend such festivities incognito, dressed as clowns or face painters, so as not to spoil their reputation or stain their virtue. "The Seánies were the surprise package, I'll tell ye, and they really stole the show. With their sing-alongs, they got the crowds goin'.

"They certainly put it up to Nobo and the boys to put on the show of their lives. And where would you leave Up With People. By Christ, The Osmonds and The Jacksons could learn a thing or two from them. Mighty stuff," raved the Dong, all smiles and backslapping.

When, a fortnight later, the Dong's emissaries put out word of a pending Rainbow Revolt, the people of the Dongdom were outraged. With times so good and things going so well, who would dare rain on their parade, the people complained. It quickly became the talk of the taverns. 'Work Will Set You Free', the Dong's posters had promised, and who could deny it. With the Twin Towers of Power nearing completion, the Dong reigned supreme and his people prospered. The Druids preached from the pulpits that the gods would show no mercy to any man, mouse or mammoth who dared disturb the natural order, in order to spoil or steal the welfare of their great nation. There would be holy war and hell to pay for any upstarts or uprisers. The Dong, the congregations were told, had the Druids' blessing to do his best for the common good and the common man.

The Dong, naturally, had the Druids exactly where he wanted them. There was nothing like holy war to mend bridges, fix fences and send the flock flying back to the fold, after the flippant folly of their ways. No black sheep here. Before he moved to declare a state of emergency and spread fears of a famine and drought (which he would pre-empt and prevent by rationing), he would first stage the World Games, so as to once again entrance the minds of the masses and display the power and prowess of the Dongdom's finest. The food shortages could then be conveniently laid at the table of the Rainbow rebels.

"With the people baying for blood, can conscription be far behind?" the Dong asked archly, before toasting Zako, who had returned from poisoning the sacred waters in the Black Pond of Świętokrzyski. With the Buddha in 'safe hands', as the Dong like to put it, and soon to spill the beans on the whereabouts of the Rainbow reservoirs and reservations, everything was falling into place. Once the children took ill from sipping the waters of Świętokrzyski, the witches and their cronies would be shortly on the run and unable to interfere.

"Sláinte, Kampai, Saúde, Chin Chin, Na Zdrowie, Cheers," the Dong raised his goblet again to Zako, who seemed a little less enthusiastic. His hesitancy was something not lost on the King, who had ordained that they would once again contest the World Games together. The climax was always the cliff diving, of which the Dong was the undisputed champion. When it came to diving into the Serpent's Hole, there was no one who could best the Dong. Zako, nevertheless, always finished a close second. On this occasion, the Dong thought he would allow his brother win. Might cheer the moody bugger up, he reckoned to himself.

The cliff diving was the most revered and feared of all the contests at the World Games, staged every four years on the Aran Islands. The diving was the most spectacular and most lethal of all the challenges. "The cliff diving is deadly," the Dong would pronounce, nodding his head, lips pursed in mock sincerity. There was telltale laughter dancing in his eyes, however, when another unfortunate misjudged his 100-feet perilous descent towards the Serpent's Hole, a coffin-shaped opening chiselled out of the craggy rock by the relentless Atlantic storms. Folklore had it that the blowhole was the door to a labyrinth, which in winter became the lair of one of the most fearsome creatures of the ocean.

Turning to Zako now, King Dong warned, "They will literally come to the ends of the earth, and then go to the ends of the earth, to beat us, Zako, but they will never edge us out." On this occasion, the Dong knew full well that he would have to finally seal the deal with the Fir Bolg at their fort at Inishmore, in order to get them onside for when the eventual confrontation happened. "Two birds with the one stone; I love it," he thought out loud. Zako said nothing. "Let's go and check on our honoured house guest, brother," proposed the Dong, letting back the last of the wine in his cup as he belched and bellowed for another jug. Arm in arm, they swigged and staggered for the north tower.

Chapter XIII

Brothers in Arms

'When I was a young man I carried me pack,
And I lived the free life of a rover.
From the Murray's green basin to the dusty outback,
I waltzed my Maltida all over.'

You cannot choose your family. You can choose your friends and, more importantly, you certainly could choose your in-laws. On all these accounts, King Dong counted himself most fortunate. He had an adoring, loving and obedient wife, who pandered to his every pleasure and had, most recently, borne him a son, as yet unnamed and heir to the throne. This son would be the next Dong and he would pronounce it so and have him blessed and named on his triumphant homecoming and victory in the war, this war to end all wars.

As for friends, the Dong chose to have none. He said, when pressed, that it avoided disappointment all round – them in him and him in them. Despite this, he was certain that he would make a great friend to someone, were he to bother. His brother Zako was different. Zako was blood, Zako was family and family mattered. In terms of enemies, the Dong liked to pick them personally and then pick on them. In this regard, it clearly helped to have four warlord brothers-in-law, who on countless occasions had been his greatest allies and brothers-in-arms. The Dong counted himself blessed with his brothers-in-law.

Married to the most famous and beautiful four sisters in the land, these brothers-in-law had united like no family and no nation before to rule the extent of the earth. North, south, east and west was their domain and, although challenged from time to time, what unfolded were mere skirmishes, started by scalds of upstarts. There was nothing in their past to measure up to the scale of what lay ahead: their finest hour, their greatest victory, a chance at long last to rout those peace-loving, tree-hugging, tea-sipping Rainbow rats. If they were so keen to travel, the Dong and his cohorts would dispatch them and all belonging to them on their final journey. They had better make the most of their Rainbow Gatherings, full moon parties and electric picnics. This would be the last war. The mother of all wars. The mother and father of all battles. The war to end all wars.

"They can have their free love, but there's no such thing as a free lunch!" The Dong roared this without warning, pounding the banquet table and almost pile-driving his fist through the teak, when one of his former special advisors had suggested trying to reason with the Rainbow Travellers, explain the plight and predicament of the Dongdom and ask them to share their resources.

"Do you think that if they dance half-naked in the moonlight, fornicate freely in the sun, and say they can walk on water, sip dandelion and daisy tea and drink nettle soup, they would ever even consider sharing a cup of cold water or mashed colcannon spuds with us? You want your head examined, man," the Dong spoke through gritted teeth. As he saw it, there were no credible objections or suitable alternatives to the path he proposed to pursue.

"Also, don't forget their yoga posturing," he added, over-egging the pudding for good measure, lest there were any lingering doubts. "Yoga posturing; men and women bending their bodies in all sorts of shapes and contortions, all possible positions, upside down and inside out and sideways; feet and toes all over the shop. And for what purpose? For snug-fitting leggings, belts and gadgets? Heads hanging down, looking backways and god-knows-where? Posturing, posturing I tell you; nothing more! Can they not just jog like everyone else?" These Rainbow People were not the butterflies they pictured themselves to be. They were more like slugs, the Dong thought with a sigh. Well, he had just the solution for them. A final solution.

$$\sharp \downarrow \gamma \maltese$$

Layla, Lola, Li Li and Lulu were the four sisters who married the warlords, and it wasn't for nothing that they were regarded as the finest women in the land. You'd have to see them for yourself to understand. They were so graceful, gregarious, gorgeous and chic that they say even Helen of Troy, Cleopatra, Gráinne Seoige and Gráinne Uaille herself shunned their company.

Lulu was the Dong's wife, and when he wasn't mad at her, he was mad about her.

Layla was married to Kamehameha the Great, Chief of Hawaii and the most feared warrior in all of Polynesia. He was regarded as the best man to handle an outrigger canoe on the entire Pacific Rim and there was no go-back in him once a fight started. If Kamehameha was a fierce fighter, he was also a fierce man for the women, but fair on both accounts. He loved and treated all his wives and girlfriends equally. In battle, he offered and expected no quarter. His foes knew that if they met him in the field they would die. Legend was that Kamehameha was the only man to ever lift the 5,000-pound Naha Stone and that he did so as a young teenager. He had to be strong, as he was fighting for his life since the day of his birth.

Chief Alapaʻinuiakauaua, on the advice of his kahuna, ordered the death of the infant great-grandson of Keaweikekahialiʻiokamoku, as his stars were a portent of a killer of chiefs. Smuggled to safety, Kamehameha was later to prove his greatness when he created the first written law in the history of Hawaii, the Mamlahoe Kanawai, the Law of the Splintered Paddle, which guaranteed the safe passage of non-combatants and saved countless lives.

Kamehameha's decree was inspired by personal experience. In one of his earliest forays, Kamehameha, in a raid on a rival ruler, trapped his foot in a rock during a beach incursion. Two fishermen from the island under attack, fearing for their lives, took the opportunity to skull Kamehameha with a large paddle, which broke from the stunning blow. The fishermen fled, leaving him for dead. Years later, the same fishermen were brought before King Kamehameha for punishment, only to be pardoned, adorned with lei and gifted land. All this unnerved the Dong, who saw it as a sign that his brother-in-law was going soft, something he attributed to him eating too many pineapples and coconuts and not enough rabbit and spuds, which put hair on your chest.

Dong longed instead to see the man who had cornered his arch-enemy Kalanikupule in the Battle of Nuʻuanu Pali, after landing his 1,200 war canoes and 10,000 warriors at Waiʻalae and Waikiki on Oʻahu. Although sustaining initial heavy losses due to treachery by a high-ranking aliʻi Kaʻiana, Kamehameha's forces bravely rallied and cunningly outflanked the opposing army before surrounding them and, in the bloody battle that ensued, killed Kalanikupule's forces to the man. Over 400 of them alone were flung from the 1,000-foot-high Pali's clifftop. Kalanikupule himself was captured and sacrificed to Kuka'ilimoku. Kamehameha was a man to have on your side in a scrap alright. The Dong liked drinking with him, but was a tinchy bit wary too, as the Hawaiian went nowhere without a supply of coconuts and his silly-looking ukulele. He even spoke once of being able to walk on water. Still, better to have him with you than against you.

Kiyomasa Katō, Li Li's husband (or Lee Lee, as she was now known in the land of the rising sun), was not to be toyed with. He was yet a boy when he cut his teeth in the Battles of Yamazaki and Shizugatake. Kiyomasa was rewarded for his loyalty and brave conduct with the revenue of 3,000 koku by the powerful Kampaku, Toyotomi Hideyoshi. Kiyomasa knew only one way – his way. He was the most sadistic of the Seven Spears of Shizugatake, the regent's feared enforcers. There was no temple, no torment beyond him, and as he continued to rise through the ranks, he was soon bestowed 250,000 koku of land. This amounted to half of all Higo province and it was received by Kiyomasa after it was confiscated from Sassa Narimassa, a far cry from his humble origins and the revenue of 170 koku.

Kiyomasa was a samurai soldier first and last and had no truck or time for wimps or weakness. The only arts he entertained were martial arts and he forbade outright the recitation of poetry in public. The only culture he would tolerate was agriculture, for peasants of course. From his residence in Kumamoto Castle, he led the extermination of all tigers in his vast domain, a matter for which he was held in high esteem by farmer and foe alike. He allowed an annual Tora Taiji, tiger-killing pageant in his honour, among other mikoshi processions, to appeal for prosperity and purification and to protect from peril and pestilence.

It was during the Seven Year War against the Korean dynasty of Joseon that Kiyomasa's legend grew. He excelled in the art of combat and the construction of castles, which often resulted in him repelling raids. He was frequently greatly outnumbered, such as when the Sino-Korean allies encircled Ulsan, after he had already captured Seoul and Busan. During the Korean campaign, Konishi Yukinaga, surrounded by a superior force, attempted to negotiate a peace treaty. The surrender bid so infuriated Kiyomasa that he swore vengeance on his fellow daimyo, which he soon fulfilled on his return to Japan. No surrender. That was the Dong's kind of soldier.

Kiyomasa, unfortunately, generally had no grá for gaijin, and would sooner skin them alive as he would a tiger. It is reputed that at the Battle of Honda, he ordered his men to cut open the bellies of all pregnant women and slice off their babies' heads. The Dong also liked drinking with him. The last chance they had gotten for a good session was on their wedding day and the Dong still recalled that hangover with affection. Kiyomasa had kindly presented him with his own signed, bamboo-embossed copy of The Art of War. Decent out, decent out altogether, the Dong recalled. Kiyomasa's gift had certainly put that duck-egg blue ukulele and those fluorescent lion figurines he had received from the other pair in the penny ha'penny place. The presence of Kiyomasa by his side was sure to put the fear of god in the Rainbow Nation. They would soon learn that there are fates worse than death.

Gustavus Adolphus, meanwhile, was the Dong's third brother-in-law, married to Lola. He wouldn't fight his way out of a paper bag and hadn't hands to scratch himself with. But the Dong again liked drinking with him and what he lacked in the field, he more than made up for it in finance. Here was a man who knew how to wage war while others paid for it. The Scandinavian King was not shy in spending the spondulicks, if there was a scrap or skirmish that needed seeing to. Despite Sweden's costly squabble with Poland, not to mention being sucked into the Thirty Year War to aid the Prussians, Gustavus, being the king that he was, was more than game to give the Dong a dig out with these Rainbow rabble. God knows, next thing you know, they'd be teaming up with the Spanish and you'd have another world war on your hands before you knew it.

Despite losing a squadron of frigates in a storm while cruising off the Bay of Riga, as well as shipping heavy losses when outmanoeuvred in the Battle of Oliwa, King Gustavus wasn't going to short-change the Dong and come up empty-handed. True, he could not dispatch three of his largest and finest ships – Tigern, Solen and Kristina – as they had been sunk by the Poles, scuttled by the crew and wrecked by a storm in the Gulf of Danzig in turn. Gustavus pledged to dig deep and he would build a maritime vessel greater than any.

The 'Vasa', as it was to be called, would vanquish enemies and wreak havoc on the high seas, sending seamen scurrying from her bulk and broadside. Time was against him, however, he told the Dong, and it would be a titanic task, but he would build him the best battleship ever to sail. The Vasa would be the scourge of their enemies and there would be no hiding place, no ocean vast enough to flee from its might.

The Dong was delighted. He didn't want this dust-up with the Rainbow People to drag on. It should be fast and furious; a lightning war. "They need another great tragedy, followed by a famous victory to remember me by," he confided in Zako. The die was cast and everything was falling nicely into place. Soon, the resources and reservoirs of the Rainbow would be under his reign. Victory was assured, that was a racing certainty. The only issue was how long the war would last, how many lives would be lost. He had lots of cannon fodder, but not so much food and even less water to spare on a convoluted campaign.

This ship was the job. The final piece in the jigsaw might bring that Buddha's heart and mind into step in jig time. Many lives would be spared (not that the Dong really cared) but could the meddling monk not trade a few maps and charts to save their souls and his soldiers, the King wondered. Let's see the Solomon in sandals consider that conundrum. Once the Rainbow rabble-rousers were routed, he would round up their ragtag remnants until they were boxed in across that hilly bogland known as the Burren. There would be no escape. Nowhere to run to, nowhere to hide.

Those who did not surrender as slaves would be pushed from the land, forced over the cliffs to perish in the awaiting Atlantic, a fitting finale as they fell off the ends of the earth. The end of the Rainbow. There would be no survivors, no heroic escapes – the Vasa would see to that as it cruised the straits between the mainland and the Aran Islands. Any stragglers in the surf would be seen to by Gustavus' Swedish marines, in a manoeuvre that Kamehameha would surely commend as his own.

"Now Zako, let us go and appraise the Buddha of our plans. Let him suck on that scape and see how many souls he's willing to squander on his self-righteousness." As Dong and Zako walked, the palace halls reverberated with the sound of their rapid footsteps.

CHAPTER XIV

Paddy's Day

'I didn't know God made honky tonk angels
I might have known you'd never make a wife
You gave up the only one that ever loved you
And went back to the wild side of life.'

To say that the Dong got a surprise when he entered the quarters he had set aside for the Buddha is not to do justice to the swirling feeling in the pit of his stomach, the dizziness running around inside his skull, the weakness in his knees, the blurring of his eyes, the welling up of anger until it led to a pain in his chest and a tightness around his throat. It all happened in a matter of moments.

No, the shock which trembled through his body and throughout the room was already echoing around the White Cities of Babylon, leaping on whispers. The shockwaves would soon be felt not just throughout the Dongdom, but they would sound around the world and throughout history itself. The disappearance of the Buddha was not just bad news for the Dong, but bad news for everyone.

It was as if the Dong, at the height of his might, had somehow, inexplicably, marginally misjudged the dive from the cliff-top into the Serpent's Hole (known as Pól An Péist – the hole of the worm – in Gaelic on the islands). As if a gentle gust served to nudge him just slightly off course as he plunged towards the ocean. Or as if some black magic...yes more likely this travesty was to blame, as the Dong would never misgauge which way the wind was blowing. It was as if, by some surreptitious voodoo, the Serpent's Hole moved a fraction as he headed for the gap between life and death. You can imagine the shock. This Buddha pest would have to pay, and pay dearly he would. Where had the Dong slipped up? There were a dozen sentries from his Republican Guard at the reinforced oak door, which offered the only access to the room.

$$\dagger \; \dagger \; \dagger \; \dagger$$

Looking back, how and what happened seems academic now, as the detail is of little importance when contrasted with the train of events that were to follow. A bloody bile of rage and bitterness consumed the Dong and steered his every thought and task thereafter. Historians remain divided to this day as to what might have unfolded were the Buddha not to have disappeared from the palace and had instead stayed, perhaps succeeding in placating the Dong in some way on that fateful evening in late February or early March.

From ancient manuscripts amassed by museums over the millennia, it is possible to reasonably accurately piece together what occurred. Suffice to say at this juncture that it drove the Dong stone-wall mad.

Now, the Dong wasn't a devout or a superstitious man, but he was not keen on taking any more chances. He summoned his top Druids, who ordained that forty days of fasting, penance and prayer be instituted to beg forgiveness and seek favour with the gods. Things had been going too well; he should have known better, but how could he possibly keep an eye on everything? The Towers of Power, White Cities of Babylon, Valentine's Day Concert, refurbishment of the Gardens of Remembrance, the World Games, the Rainbow rebels, the witches, the Buddha, the media, the war effort, the fundraising, the Senate – they were all pulling out of him and the water, the water, the water and the leaks and the leaks from the Senate and the drip-drip of information from the Republican Guard about the mysterious disappearance of the Buddha of Ballyhuppahaun were enough to drive him to distraction.

Where were his special advisors when he needed them? They didn't see this coming. No one saw this coming. He was acting on best advice, the best advice available from the best brains in the land. They didn't see it coming, so how could he? In future, he would take their best advice with a pinch of salt. The worst, he instinctively knew, was yet to come. The Dong wasn't a superstitious man, but he knew bad things came in threes and so they did. Well, not really in threes, because they didn't stop at three and just when he thought things couldn't get any worse, they did.

The very next morning a contingent of Kamehameha's men arrived, exhausted as they had sailed and paddled for weeks without once stopping.

Their leader, Paiea, which means hard-shelled crab – and this sturdy boy did resemble a crab standing upright – had more bad news to deliver. He revealed that, even as Kamehameha had secretly prepared a war party to dispatch to line-up alongside the Dong's forces, the gods had intervened. As he blooded the warriors in a skirmish in Puna district, misfortune struck in their pursual of the rival chief Keoua. As he and his band fled past the Kilauea volcano, it erupted and killed nearly half of his warriors from poisonous gas.

Undeterred by this minor setback, Kamehameha pressed on, but as he tried to assert his control to the two remaining islands west of O'ahu and outside his domain, namely Kaua'i and Ni'ihau, more problems erupted. As he set out from Honolulu to finally bring Kaumualii 'i, ali 'i nui of Kaua'i to heel, Ka'iana's brother Namakeha led a rebellion on Hawaii island and King Kamehameha was currently preoccupied with putting down the insurrection. The Dong was getting a headache trying to follow it all, and lost track of just who was attacking who on what island. He was about to order the messenger's head off until he had second thoughts. It could be Kamehameha's brother or cousin, for all he knew. This stocky, sallow man and his crew were also fit-looking fellows and might not go as quietly to meet their maker as the usual scrawny, breathless boys sent on such errands. The bottom line was Kamehameha could not dispatch an army at this time to help hammer the Rainbow.

"Kamehameha says to be assured that he will instead build a heiau to Kuka'ilimoku and offer an ali'i in sacrifice," Paiea prattled on, explaining that this was the advice of the big kahuna back on the main island.

"Could he not just send some money or gold instead?" asked the Senator with a snigger, as the Dong turned away in dismay. "Our wells are not the only things that are running dry," he added. The Senator stroked his salt-and-pepper beard, grimaced and thought better of pushing it any further, thanks to a deathly glance from the Dong. Surely, the Senator knew better than to be strutting his sarcasm today, the Dong thought. What had him so chirpy?

Before they could leave the great hall, the sound of the gushing fountains outside caused the Dong's tongue to stick to the roof of his mouth so badly that even his saliva seemed on strike. The Senator clapped for a jug of water, clipping the servant on the back of the lug for his tardiness in not tending to the Dong's thirst. They needed to secure those Rainbow wells or blood would flow in place of water.

As if on cue, another messenger entered. This lad had flowing blonde locks, matching handlebar whiskers and ginny-goat beard and more bandanas, bracelets, bangles, beads, belts and buckles than you'd come across after bedtime at a Rainbow traveller's triple wedding.

"Scandinavian," smirked the Senator in the Dong's ear. As smart alec and all as the Senator was, the Dong could not but agree that if this fellow about-faced, you'd take him for a whore. For one sneaky second, he could not help but picture how Gustavus' guy would fare out against Paiea and his tattooed posse from Polynesia. "Sailors," was all he could say, shaking his head and rolling his eyes to heaven. "What now? What now, Kristina?" urged the Dong, prompting general anxiety and confusion in the process. Even the Hawaiian contingent were on their hunkers in uproar. It was at risk of becoming pandemonium.

"Viksten, Viksten," growled the courier in that guttural Nordic way and the Dong, who couldn't help himself once he had an audience, feigned fear. Wide-eyed, he uttered pointedly, "I sure as hell hope your bark is worse than your bite." By now, the Hawaiians could not contain themselves.

"Listen Viksten, raise your voice to me again like that and it will be the last time you'll lace up your leggings or get a longing in a longboat, if you get my drift," the Dong warned, which quickly restored order. Zako took a single step forward so that everyone, especially the Swedish sailor, knew he was serious.

"I'm glad everyone understands we were only lightening up an otherwise dreary day because, on the trouble side of things, Zako here has secured the franchise in these parts and is soon to expand his ambit of operations as the west coast distributor. So what is it Vicky, Kristina, or are you from Barcelona? Spit it out, or have you swallowed your tongue?"

"The Vasa is sunk," Viksten's words floated round the room before they too led to that sinking feeling back in the bowels of the Dong's stomach.

"What sorcery? What sabotage? What stupidity?" The Senator took the words right out of the Dong's mouth, without permission, mind, and by the holy mother of god, if things weren't bad enough, was this politico also getting too big for his boots? You could not say he had a lean and hungry look, as this porcupine was as fat as Falstaff, larding the lean earth as he moved. The Dong determined nonetheless to beware the ides of March and struggled to keep his fury in check.

Viksten, King Gustavus Adolphus' nephew, after requesting a glass of water, sat down and set out in great detail what had happened to the Vasa. The magnificent vessel was, it turns out in hindsight, built with indecent haste in a genuine attempt to have it pressed into action at the earliest possible opportunity. Loaded to the bolts with 64 brass cannon on two gun decks, the 1,200 tonne, 226 feet long flagship saw no expense spared, costing more than 40,000 dalers at the Skeppsgarden shipyards, where it was fitted out and furnished to accommodate 145 crew and 300 royal marines, under Captain Sofring Hansson.

"Only god knows how it happened," Viksten admitted, shrugging off any superstitious speculation as to grand ship's fate. "Perhaps its keel was too shallow, its width too narrow or its ballast bungled. Its broadside, though, would blast any fleet to kingdom come. This ship was invincible, with no equal on the seven seas. My uncle Gus is inconsolable."

As the Vasa embarked on her maiden voyage, it sank in seconds. As implausible as it sounds, the haphazard hilarity of the sinking was seen by thousands of spectators on the shore in Stockholm, who had turned out to glimpse the massive battleship with their own eyes as it moved down the archipelago from Skeppsgarden to the naval station at Alvsnabben. The water was dead calm. The Vasa only struggled to catch a puff of a gentle southwest breeze to fluff out its three sails set. The gun ports were open, prepared to fire a celebratory salute as the ship left harbour. The Vasa never got to shoot off a single volley, however. As it emerged from the lee of the city, a gust filled her sails and she heeled suddenly to port side, the salty brine gushing through the open lower gun ports. She listed further and Captain Sofring's frantic orders could not save the Vasa and the three dozen souls who perished in 100 feet of water, only 400 feet from shore. With survivors clinging to debris to save themselves, the ship's fore-topgallant mast still jutted above the surface, a sailor impaled on it, as if it were a crucifix to mark the spot.

"I would not believe it if I had not seen it for myself with my own two eyes." Viksten sounded every bit as broken-hearted by the affair as his uncle.

If all of this seemed a trifle farfetched, the sceptical would never believe what actually happened next. It was, after all, as the Dong was at pains to confirm, Friday, March 13th.

With the ranks in the room sweaty and swollen, between soldiers and messengers in the unseasonal humidity, a racing pigeon fluttered to the floor, exhausted, gasping. Small wonder, as it had just flown non-stop from Japan, not only with a note clipped to its left leg but in full samurai-style body armour and headgear.

"Tell me this is dream; a nightmare from which I will awaken at the count of three," pleaded the Dong to the assembly, as he still reeled, in a daze from the horror of the Buddha's disappearance and the ensuing shambles.

The pigeon who had defied peregrine, merlin, kestrel, harriers, hawks and buzzards was almost beaten for want of water, which thankfully was put to rights by Viksten, who shared the drops of water in his cup with the collared dove. Having drunk some, it at once puffed out its chest, did a short, sharp strut, followed by a quick flutter to formally announce its arrival.

The note. From Katō, of course. This was going to be special, the Dong presumed, as he struggled to roll out the tiny parchment between his index fingers and thumbs. When he finally got the paper to heed, he looked at it, puzzled and frustrated by the complex script, slowly shaking his head from side to side, as he held his breath to contain himself. He then handed over the offending hieroglyphics to the Senator. The Senator, on the other hand, appeared extraordinarily phlegmatic considering the circumstances, his nonchalance only serving to irk the Dong even further. The King decided to let the hare sit for now. There would be no rash beheadings; he had enough on his plate. In any event, he needed the Senator to decipher this bloody note.

The Senator, there was no denying it, was a cute hoor and had been about many towns. He was well-travelled, having been to places as far flung as Tokyo, Timbuktu, Tobercurry and even Timahoe. He would, no doubt, make a meal of this, with ink and quill and pomp and paraphernalia. Another day lost, and not a sinner dead on the battlefield; everything at a standstill for a few scribbles on a letter delivered by a pigeon. The Dong was beside himself with rage and had to concentrate on breathing so as not to hyperventilate and go into convulsions, for the time being anyway.

Hours later, the Japanese hiragana and katakana symbols were deciphered. Ikenai. Ryu wo oikaketeru kara. Tsuishin honto ni gomen nasai. 行けない。　龍を追いかけてるから。　追伸　本当にごめんなさい。

The Senator, seemingly somewhat less full of beans now, tentatively handed over his own transcribed note to the Dong. CAN'T COME. CHASING THE DRAGON. PS. SO SORRY. Speechless and in disbelief, the Dong stormed from the room and headed for his inner sanctum, with only Zako and the Senator daring to follow. There wasn't a ha'p'orth either of them could say. This was bad. All bad. Any prospects for peace, truce or treaty were gone, out the door. Only the scale of the slaughter remained at issue. Years of welling anger and resentment towards the Rainbow People would finally be given full vent, in the guise of just cause; a crusade to restore order and reclaim what was rightly theirs to begin with, the very water of life itself and who would dare judge any wrong in that? Soon, a drought would grip the land and it would wring the last drop of compassion from the soul of even holy men. For water to flow, blood would have to flow. That was easy enough for even a fool to follow.

As feared by the pair who stood by him, the Dong went straight for the secret vaults to break open the war chest. Sensing faint protest in their hearts, he paused. "Is it not better to save it until there's no other option? We have sufficient armies and allies to suppress the Rainbow and prevail. Best keep it for a rainy day," chanced Zako, more pleadingly than with conviction.

"Senator, could you go to the window and tell me what you see?" the Dong asked.

"The sun splitting the trees," the Senator responded, puzzled.

"Fair play, an iota of honesty from a politico. The sun splitting the trees in March. My wife cold on a slab. My son, yet without a name, kidnapped for the Rainbow to hold me to ransom and revelling in it with carry-on, cavorting and carnivals. If that's not a bloody rainy day then when will there ever be one?" The Dong was raising the roof, the full extent of their new predicament only now dawning on all when he put it like that.

"'Chasing the Dragon', I ask ye. Summon Boonyon of the Fir Bolg and arrange a parley with the Dogs of War. Sun Tzu must be turning in his grave. I should never have underestimated my enemies and will never again overestimate my friends and allies. Money may not buy love, but there will be no love lost for what I have in mind. Mercenaries. Contractors in death, the most ruthless men ever born. Yes, we have millions of foot soldiers, loyal and brave, who will fight to the death. I will accommodate their wishes too. Make no mistake: there's a big difference between not being afraid to die and not being afraid to kill." The Dong was like a new man. A man possessed. A driven demon, hell-bent on revenge. His mission in life, he said, was finally clear. The fog of procrastination had lifted; he must save mankind.

"Save mankind from himself at all cost," Dong shouted out. Yes, there would be a bloody war, but it would be no drawn-out affair, with years of suffering and deprivation. He would heroically sacrifice himself and his family if need be for an early victory. This war, he promised, would be short and sweet.

Dong ordered Zako back to the plains of Świętokrzyski, this time to personally finish off the witches and their consorts. The Senator was ordered north, to tie up any loose ends with the hitherto banished Fir Bolg and to hammer out a deal with the Dogs of War, at a rendezvous in Dunluce Castle. First, however, they were made wait for one other task.

"Send in the farmer," the Dong demanded. Paddy Murphy, the farmer, explained that he wasn't really a farmer but a carpenter who did a small bit of sheep farming on the side, for which he assured by the Senator that there were no tax implications.

"I'm an honest man." Murphy continued by claiming that, while from the south, his jobbing took him to all sorts and all sorts of places. He was not a man given to loose talk, idle banter, slander, gossip or the like. He seldom if ever put his foot in his mouth.

"I'm an honourable man." Murphy felt it his duty to the state and for the common good (he was, after all, a mere commoner who, as he had already said, did a small bit of sheep farming on the side), to relate what he had seen. While seeking out conacre and spring lambs, he stumbled on shocking shenanigans across the way in Świętokrzyski.

"What did I tell ye, Zako? Didn't I warn you many's the time about that Grażyna, Gráinne and Gemma ones, and their gang plain gallivanting and up to no good," the Dong said, rubbing it in, for he knew full well that Zako had a soft spot for them and this would put paid to all that, once and for all.

"Well," Murphy went on, "they were foolin' around, foostering about, play-acting and frolicking with those rowdy, bawdy foul-mouthed Fomorians all week, round Valentine's back there. It was bang out of order and all them poor children then falling sick after being poisoned from the water of the Black Ponds and their poor parents demented. It was clear to me on the full moon that them girls were up to no good, running round ring-a-ring-a-rosy in the nip and skinny dippin' in the lakes. No good could come of it and sure we all know what happened – aren't the children sick out since."

"A saintly man, a pure saint; that's what you are and to use your own words, thems no girls, they're witches out," Dong replied warmly. "What you saw was black magic, snakes of Fomorians and sinners of easy women and brave you are to break your silence, to come forward and expose them for the what they are – pure evil." As the Dong continued his commentary, the Senator and Zako looked stunned and strung out, rattled by the day's events.

"Grotesque, unbelievable, bizarre and unprecedented." The Dong, it seemed, was reading their minds, himself electrified. The more the plot thickened, the more he liked it; the more he rose to the occasion.

"Step forwards, sheep farmer. Small or not, you're a shepherd of men. You have saved souls, countless souls. You didn't shirk; you stepped up when it came to saving your flock, as the wolves circled and howled at the moon. A saint of a man and henceforth we shall celebrate your selflessness and I will immediately command a new public holiday. A day to celebrate the common man, 'Paddy's Day'. A day forevermore of music and merriment, to commemorate the testimony of a small sheep farmer and the day we ran the snakes of Fomorians and their flirtatious, foreign-fetish-loving female enchantresses from this isle. I'll give them ring-a-ring-a-rosy. What a day it's been, but what a day it's going to be, Paddy. Chasing the Dragon, Paddy's Day."

Chapter XV

Enter the Dragon

'Trouble, trouble.
I try to chase trouble but it's chasing me.
Trouble, trouble.
Trouble with a capital T.'

"Zugzwang!" swore the Buddha, who seldom swore. "Zugzwang, Zugzwang, Zugzwang. Bad, bad move." He stomped for a bit, before remembering that he had the infant wrapped up beneath his coat. Peeling back the layers, the baby boy peered back, cooing and giggling, sucking on the edge of the blanket. Even in the half dark, his eyes looked straight into you, in the disarming way that babies do – too close for comfort, their helplessness being their overpowering strength.

The Buddha had to check himself from purring back as the boy made eye contact. He seemed to look into his very soul with (as the Buddha noticed for the first time) one pale blue eye, while the other eye was tinted blue with speckled triangles of green and brown. The Buddha felt as though he knew that look, as sure as if he had stared into those very eyes a thousand times before, each time more beguiling and entrancing than the last. Bad move or not, there was no turning away or turning back this time.

The Buddha made for the Forest of the Giant Bonsais. Scarcely known of – and those who did avoided it like the plague –, it would be safe to hold up there and make a plan to get the child into safe hands before making haste to the Rainbow clans. The Forest of the Giant Bonsais was as weird as it was wonderful. As folk seldom dared to venture there, except by chance, the place was safe once one got past the overgrowth and wilderness. At its heart, the forest was bountiful and secure from the assassins the Dong had almost definitely dispatched.

The twisted and torn giant bonsais had barks worse than their bite, the Buddha joked to himself. Nevertheless, they certainly cast an eerie shadow and, on the few occasions that soldiers, salesmen, statesman or sages from the Dongdom had strayed or ventured and dared to dally there, the witches would add fuel to the fire and fan the flames of folklore by pulling pranks with willing allies no fiercer than a few puck goats, March hares and that half-caste parrot Scobie.

Despite his heavy heart, the Buddha could still spare time for a belly laugh, which in turn the baby copy-catted, as he recalled how, one Halloween, Grażyna and her gang were up to devilment and set Scobie on an unsuspecting sage from the highest order of the saints. Off track, out of ideas and out of breath, as crispy autumn leaves had disguised his route, the sage ended up sitting down to take his soggy sandwich on the knotted brang of a bougainvillea. Little did he know he was being sized up by the motley mischief-makers, when a fork of lightning signalled a downpour so severe that it washed the dye right out of the ripe red maple leaves in the adjacent tree. If the lightning hadn't put the heart crossways in him, the blood-like droplets that fell onto his sorrowful sandwich did the trick, before the witches put the tin hat on it altogether when they sent Scobie flying down onto his shoulder to squawk, "What's the story, Scobie?" That fairly lifted him out of it, flailing and swinging his shillelagh, throwing shapes in all and every direction as he never stopped running, his feet hardly hitting the ground before he miraculously made it back to the highway; the culprits in chronic convulsions, safely concealed in the canopy.

There were no more strays to the Forest of the Giant Bonais for a long time to come, after someone as influential and as convincing as the sage Fogarty was finished filling people in on the bleeding trees and talking birds. "Now that's how rumours start," said a decidedly delirious Deirdre, who then disappeared into the bowels of the bonsai forest on the back of a big brown goat, a merry band of accomplices in tow. On especially long nights, the Buddha hankered after that belle époque, but knew full well there was no going back. They had all grown up now, moved on and a new age would have to dawn, one way or the other, for better or worse.

It was in the Forest of the Giant Bonsais that the Buddha had first learned the true nature of rain. For forty years, it had failed to even drizzle. The bonsais hung in there, as did the shrubs, in the undergrowth below, along with the briars and bluebells. The pungent dog rose's girlie pink and white flowers failed to show for season after season, as they too struggled to survive the drought. Parched, the forest called on all its reserves, still sending shoots to scout for precious precipitation. When the thunderclap finally came, it started a round of applause, lifting the listless leaves in a crescendo of appreciation; every branch, stem and leaf stretching out in a standing ovation of thanks for the downpour, which the Buddha thought could be heard around the world. To this day, the waft of a wild rose reminded the Buddha of that delightful cloudburst which had salvaged the giant bonsais. He thought of the sound of raindrops dancing to the approval of the outstretched courgette, cucumber, cabbage and cauliflower leaves, as they lap it up, beating the rhythm of life itself. There is nothing more precious than a drop of rain.

"Dukkah!" The Buddha had had a moment of enlightenment: The boy needed a name, so he would call him after his old dragon friend, Tekisui, 'drop of water'. As the original holder of the name, Tekisui the Last Dragon had gotten it thanks to his fondness of drinking water from ice-cold pools, as snowmelt cascaded down the rapids. Nothing else could quench his insatiable thirst, he said, and so Buddha nicknamed him Tekisui, a name that stuck.

Tekisui was not really the last dragon either, as there was no such thing. He was merely the last dragon to leave the natural order and move to the other side. Tekisui did so with such stubborn reluctance that he gave himself the name of The Last Dragon, on his final day in that world that one can perceive with the naked eye. He and his kind now lived peacefully and in happiness as dragonflies, without being constantly hounded and harassed. The foresaking of their former shape as fire-breathing dragons was the price they had to pay for this peaceful life.

To roam the earth, to hover and drink peacefully from its waterways, however, was a price many dragons found too harsh and too high. Others adapted more quickly and happily took to their new lives as dragonflies, colourful and free of persecution, in which they thrived and prospered. Tekisui struggled to make the move and the morph but eventually gave in to the Buddha's pleadings. They hadn't seen each other in an age.

Buddha missed Tekisui but in the end, his going over to the other side to live as a dragonfly was far better than dying as a dragon. The life of a dragonfly was free and fun, if a little less dramatic than that of a dragon. The reality was that dragons were being hunted to extinction. The reason for this was ridiculous but beside the point, as one dragon after another continued to be slain. If it went on for much longer, they all would perish and be gone for good. In light of this, and at the prompting of the Zen Masters, the Tuatha Dé Danann and the Circle of Witches, a full counsel of the Drone of Dragons was called.

The dragons' principal problem, it was established, was that they were ahead of their time. Every time a disaster unfolded in the world, the Drone of Dragons would dispatch their strongest and fiercest dragon to warn the people. Travelling faster than time, the dragons would fly ahead to warn the people, foaming and fuming at the mouth, so fast was their speed. By the time they arrived at the village or city gates they were parched with the thirst and gasping for water, so they would clear their throats of flames as they desperately tried to warn of the impending doom of dust storm, deluge, tempest or pestilence.

The startled townspeople and city folk, in fear of their lives, invariably summoned up their bravest knights to repel and vanquish the disbelieving and furious dragon, who often left in dismay, huffing and puffing. More than once, a few of them were known to shoot off a flame in the direction of county or city hall in disgust. Their message, as well-meaning and all as it might have been, was never well received or regarded, and the dragons were being hunted down day and night to the verge of extinction. Of course, what always followed was the foreseen disaster itself, hot on the heels of the dragon's foray, and this too was laid at their door, not as a coincidence but as a consequence of their unwelcome visit. This further compounded the mounting mistrust, misconceptions and misunderstanding on both sides. In the finish, no one was safe, neither dragon, day nor knight.

Although the scenario was a great pity and pitiful, the dragons ultimately agreed that a low profile was crucial and, for now at least, they had best choose a different course, leaving their mighty forms behind. They were no longer comfortable or safe in that skin and so the dragons, weary and wistful, moved on to live in harmony with nature, in lives no less important now that they were dragonflies.

Tekisui; so it would be. Lulu's boy had a name, if little else. Recollecting his current plight, the Buddha quickly became aware of how he had, unknownst to himself, drifted off again into a world of his own, as he recalled the wild days he had spent with his dragon friend. Tempus fugit, time flies, and he would have to fly himself if the little lad was to be got to safety. Time was against him too if he was to warn the Rainbow Tribes and Dinosaur Clans of the Dong's desire for all-out war. The Forest of the Giant Bonsais was bountiful and the boy would be safe here among the weird and wonderful. He would want for nothing, with friends and food for body and soul. He had pledged to Lulu though to take him to her sisters for rearing – a promise never to be taken lightly, and ever more so now.

As Tekisui took forty winks, thanks to a lemon balm potion in his bottle, the Buddha lingered for one last time, as goats grazed in clover, ignoring hares racing each other around dogwood and banyan trees, the swiftest of them stopping to gnaw on the dogwood bark, on the tippy-toes of their hind legs.

Once more, the Buddha, enjoying a cup of tea in the hand from a favourite Giant Bonsai Forest recipe, entrusted to him by an old friend and full-time resident of the forest (Mrs Furuya, or Fusa, as she insisted in being called), drifted back to that last fateful evening with Lulu. She had waited for the Senator to leave by the padlocked oak door, before slipping out of the shadows, as if by some magic. The Buddha however, hearing the soft snick of a hidden door before it glided open, knew better. Indeed, she would not have startled the Buddha had he heard nothing, as he would recognise her shape and her scent in shade or in dark. The Senator had, on the face of it, brought a cup of tea to help him sleep, and he had promised the sun, moon and stars if only the Buddha were to see sense and co-operate with the Dong and his fair quest for fresh water, food and forests.

As the Buddha had sat there, impassively and imperviously, the Senator eventually showed his true colours, warning of eternal damnation – but only after the Buddha had been first hanged, drawn and quartered. His ilk, he was warned, would fetch a similar fate and it would be all on the Buddha's head, the blood on his hands, and if any managed by some slim chance to survive, they would be scattered on the four winds, homeless, the Senator had assured him.

"I cannot give you what is neither mine nor yours to take. Neither can you, nor even the Mighty Dong, steal the sun, moon and stars and, thankfully, the sand, sea or surf on the shore for that matter," stated the Buddha, his reply driving the Senator from the room, rapid with rage.

As the Buddha made for a sip of tea for his parched lips, Lulu had slipped in beside him to press gently upon his left arm (the Buddha being a citeog) and pry the cup from his fingers before it reached his mouth. She then placed it on the stool beside the settle bed. It was only well later that the full significance of what has just happened dawned on him, as the pair got lost catching up and chatting about the old days. By way of consolation, Lulu had explained that she married the Dong for her parents and for peace sakes, and look where that landed her. There had been enough said and the Buddha left it at that. He was sorry now that he did. He agreed safe passage for the boy, without fear or favour, and they sealed that promise with a kiss. A warm kiss that had no equal, one more time, for the boy. There was no going back now and, as he dared to see and smell her for a final moment before fleeing through the hidden passageway, the Buddha was gifted an abiding smile, as Lulu lifted and, with what he only afterwards could call a knowing look, swallowed in one go the hemlock-laced tea.

Deep in the bowels of the Giant Bonsai Forest, the Buddha was face to face with Fusa Furuya, who, according to anyone who could remember that far back, had lived here forever. Mrs Furuya, who was a legend when it came to herbs and healing, readied the Buddha a concoction to "keep him safe" and a remedy for the little lad's runny nose. She would keep you chatting forever if you let her and, only she knew the Buddha was on a mission, he'd have never gotten out of her cottage.

As if he weren't apprehensive enough, her advice mystified the Buddha, as she pottered around her tiny kitchen, with its vessels and vases and incense wafting to the rafters – so much incense, in fact, that at one stage he lost sight of her altogether in the fog of frankincense fragrance, detecting Fusa only by her constant chanting. "Don't go north. Go west to go east," she advised. As he finally tried to leave, she pressed a small parcel into his arms. "Another little bundle for you," she added, ignoring the Buddha's protestations that there was no need and that she was too kind.

Fusa, however, fussily insisted, explaining that it was for her family back east. As he made tracks under the cover of darkness and departed the Forest of the Giant Bonsais, Buddha did so with the blessing of a full moon, still uncertain if Fusa's advice was sound, or the old woman had simply wanted him to let her folks know she was alive and well. Better to be safe than sorry, he supposed. He would go west to go east, but first he had treacherous terrain to cross before he made it to the Forest of the See-Through Trees, and then onwards along his journey to Japan.

With the Blue Stacks and Benbulbin to his back, the Buddha made sure to keep the Mish and Macgillycuddy Reeks hard to his heel, as he made for the Shannon Callows, The Marshes and The Fen, before heading for The Bog that skirted Ballyhuppahaun. He would cut across from Clara, Clonsast, Coolnamona and Coolrain and curl deep amid the turf. He had his hideouts here and would not be bothered, as Will O' The Wisp, the banshees and the baying elk kept most out of these parts, even on the brightest of nights. It would mean meagre rations, but little rivalled the refreshing gush of a bog spring and he had buried butter, bread and other morsels here for such an occasion. The heather would be an ample blanket, the fluffy down of the bog-cotton a cradle for the boy and the overhanging hedgerow his home, safely surrounded by a moat of forbidding bog holes.

As the Buddha set up camp in Kyletaleesha, he looked with envy upon the herd of red deer – a stag at their helm – heading back up towards Bladma, his sweet Slieve Blooms, beautiful Ballyhuppahaun and his friends that he was forced to leave behind. A startling noise through a hole in the hedge turned out to be no more than a curious hare, who tipped on in the footsteps of the deer, after he had hurriedly stood upright on his hind legs, had a look around, splashed his face in the spring pool and headed on with acknowledging nod. Although on the outskirts now of the Shadowlands, the Buddha would have no more visitors tonight.

Just then, the boy took into a bawl. Nothing would soothe him. Not even the potion from Mrs Furuya. The Buddha was clumsy in the childcare department and, in despair of a night's rest (and fit to pull his hair out) he resorted to a bedtime story. He would tell Tekisui the story of Kang, here in his arms by a gentle but honest fire on the banks of turf at Kyletaleesha, taking care not to set the heather blazing and awaken the ghosts of the Shadowlands.

"The sorry tale of Kang is sometimes better known as the story of the man-eating tiger. Kang Wannian, a villager from Mengla in Yunnan

Province, encountered a tiger while gathering freshwater clams on the Chinese-Laos border one spring. Kang and the tiger, which had no known name, did not know each other, had never met before but were to have a profound effect on each other's lives..."

The Buddha noticed, as he rocked back and fro in the soft sod, that Tekisui had stopped sobbing, so he stayed going, well pleased with himself as the boy beamed up at him, his face awash in the full moon.

"After a standoff which seemed an eternity to Kang but was surely only seconds, the two became locked in mortal combat, with Kang killing the tiger. He was only later to learn that it was the last known tiger, though without a name, in Indochina. Kang skinned and ate the tiger, with the help of four others from his village. When some high-ranking officials learned of Kang's tiger feast, he was at once arrested and sentenced to ten years in prison with hard labour for killing a rare animal, the last tiger in Indochina.

"Kang vigorously protested his innocence, claiming self-defence. The court also sentenced his accomplices, who helped Kang dismember and eat the tiger, to four years for covering up and concealing their criminal gains. Kang was also fined 480,000 yuan. Kang's downfall in his defence was that he had carried a pistol, which gave him the edge when it came to dispatching the lunging tiger. Prosecutors avowed that Kang did not need a gun to gather clams. So Kang's last supper as a free man was the last tiger of Pangtang, as it is believed that that is where the tiger was born, although he perished far away from home.

"What is the moral of the story of the man-eating tiger, Tekisui? Let me tell you so, as I sense some ignorance in your silence. Is Kang ultimately the cause of the tigers' fate, as he did, after all, only eat one tiger and that in self-defence? Surely, the man who killed the first tiger is equally to blame for its extinction. Should they also be found, fined and jailed? Perhaps all these questions we can put to your uncle Kiyomasa, when we get to Japan.

"Then again, perhaps not, as the irony of the story might not impress a soldier such as himself, as much as it does us scholars and men of the world," said the Buddha, pausing. Tekisui was sound asleep. The Buddha did not know for how long, or how much of the story the boy had missed.

He would have to recount the yarn of the man-eating tiger for him again at some later stage. It certainly had proved a more potent parable than even Mrs Furuya's potion.

The Buddha knew they had come to the border of the Shadowlands when they encountered the buachalans, scavanagers and grey crows. Beyond lay only ramshackle huts, empty houses and shells of dwellings, which doubled as homes for the palefaced folk that haunted them. The mercurial sky constantly threatened a downpour, though it never really rained more than a pathetic drizzle. From this distance, the buildings, matching the demeanour of the clouds, looked as if they were cavernous grey pumpkins, which had their eyes and teeth roughly gouged out and were plonked there randomly, as if temporary shelters, shacks and shanties.

The Buddha prepared to make a burst for the Forest of the Sea-Through Trees. He hugged the hedgerows hemming the bogland, struck by how the honeysuckle buzzed with life. The hazel, hawthorn and holly were all heavily pregnant with a bounty of nuts and berries, reaching out above the strong scented yarrow, with its feathered flowers and stingy nettles standing sentry. More than once, the Buddha had relied on them all to tend a wound or fill his belly. Their presence signalled a long, hard winter in the Shadowlands, but no one tended the stony grey soil, which had migrated here too from Monaghan and Outer Mongolia.

Blow-ins, they were branded by the natives, and got as friendly a welcome as dandelion fluff on the wind. Sowing seeds was vieux jeu in the Shadowlands. For a moment, up ahead in the distance, the Buddha thought he spied some scarecrows – a good sign, he figured. On closer inspection however, it turned out to be only people standing still, talking and not tilling. No scarecrows need apply for work on this sprawling estate. They had better move along, get along, go, move, shift. Frightened scarecrows: scary, thought the Buddha. The Shadowlanders had no time to sow and so ended up with no time; no time for anything, not even time for each other. At this rate, they would soon run out of time altogether. No work for scarecrows; that said enough.

It was easier to make it through the Shadowlands than you might think. The Buddha devised to pull up his hoodie, keep his head down and make out like a beggar with a baby. No one in the Shadowlands batted an eyelid or paid a blind bit of heed. By nightfall, they were among friends.

The Buddha would rot you, going on and on about the Forest of the See-Through Trees. He would call it The Rainbow Forest. And sure enough, there were rainbows left, right and centre. As you washed, walked or worked, rainbows would appear on your face, your foot, your fingers, your chin and your cheeks – all four of them. Rainbows everywhere, so it really should have been called The Rainbow Forest in the first place.

It was a great opportunity to catch up and swap stories with all the Rainbow Travellers who converged here. The forest was alive with all sorts of streams and creatures, of which the unicorn seemed the most mundane. Rainbow fruit and flowers were delicious and delightful; rainbow birds, butterflies, red squirrels and red-faced cherubs hung out in the see-through trees. As rain ran down inside and out, like downpipes the translucent timber trunks held droplets that prismatically refracted, reflected and projected the sun's rays as rainbows. They were everywhere, until even lilywhite goats and fluffy fawn hares were painted top to tail like zebras, but in lines of red, orange, yellow, green, blue, indigo and violet, as they stepped in and out of the sun. It was fierce craic, as the forest was awash with rainbows big and small. You'd find them in places you'd least expect.

One of the Buddha's favourite pastimes was to sit out along, as far as it would bear, a skinny, see-through branch, reading his book to passers-by, apparently sitting on thin air, as the bough was invisible from the angle they were looking from. For further amusement, flocks of goliath birdwing, tortoiseshell, peacock, dogface and tiger swallowtail butterflies would tickle and torment, as they licked salt from any bare skin. Meanwhile, the Buddha's buddy, Stevo Da Shaman, wrestled with a slippy tree as he tried to shin up the slithery bark. He was blissfully unaware of the rainbow streak down his head and back, which gave him a hilarious technicoloured mane, as the man made a monkey of himself, failing miserably to make any headway as he constantly slid back down, ending up on his bruised rump.

Sorer was Stevo's bruised ego, but it was nothing that a refreshing pint of elderflower cordial wouldn't cure, and where better to fizz the concoction than in the rapid streams of the Rainbow Forest, as the pair plotted for supper al fresco with guests on the banks of the River Rio. Buddha couldn't wait to see their faces when he presented the mighty Tekisui. Among them would be Nana (who was called after her favourite singer of all time, Nana Mouskouri), Nina, Tryna and Nino, Kathy and Dee, Attie, Jas, Magnum, Pee Pee (who was an uncle of the Buddha's), Cosby, Seymour and Si.

Si was a legend on the didgeridoo. They had just landed and, much to the Buddha's satisfaction, had brought with them special dukkah they had gotten from a voyager wizard in Oz. "Sweet," the Buddha said, blessing them both. They were a sight for sore eyes after their long journey. "Sweet," echoed Stevo, who made the mistake of saying he was looking forward to his lemonade, only to be chastised by the Buddha, who pointed out that it was pure elderflower cordial and good for you.

"So, what's for supper so?" queried Si, the butterflies having a field day on his salty forearms as the sweat oozed out of him.

"It's a surprise, lots of surprises," the Buddha replied, giving away nothing except lots of elderflower cordial to pacify the parched Rainbow travellers. The Buddha loved the Rainbow Forest and on days like this wished he never had to leave. It wasn't just the rillions of rainbows decorating every inch of the forest; the sunflowers here always delighted and gave him butterflies in his belly as they stretched out to the heavens to try and tip the stars. He wondered if his old friend Ever Ramirez had stopped climbing yet. Had he made it to the top and would he ever see him again?

As for the stars themselves, one can just imagine how they radiated, romped and tumbled amid the see-through trees, when they came out to tease the sunflowers once the evenings were beat. Even the night sky in Mazury and Ballyhuppahaun could not at their best boast as many stars. This was the greatest show on earth – well, after Clonaslee, according to the Buddha, who would never concede any ground on that score. Most importantly in the Rainbow Forest, his fellow travellers would be here. He could learn, they would listen, and together they would laugh. Yes, the place was awash with rainbows but, best of all, everything here was clear. You could see the wood from the trees. In the Rainbow Forest you could always come and go; you were free. Free to surf, free to read, free to grow seeds, free to dive, free to surface, free to ride, free to stand still, free to do yoga or just stand on your head, if you preferred. Always free to do something.

The Buddha knew he needed to loosen up a little. As a pair of cheeky cherubs (herding puck goats while riding around on a big black jack-ass, flecked and dashed in broken rainbow parts) had offered to take Tekisui off his hands for the day, the Buddha thought it time to fit in a little yoga, followed by a few sun salutations. That would do the trick before setting about dinner.

Don't forget to breathe, he reminded himself, as his thoughts rambled lazily to Grażyna, Gráinne, Gemma and the witches. He also thought of Dodo – his best friend – his surfing mates and soul pals on big swell days, great hurling matches, sing-songs and drumming sessions to beat the band, beside a hearty, open fire. He wondered would he ever see them again. Who would warn the witches if he did not make it back?

The Dong was on the warpath and this would end in tears. Buddha had implored Dodo to head for the hills, to Hippy Bill's, and to hang out with the surfers in Dooey until it was safe to roam and return home. Dodo had kicked up a fuss something shocking, full of futile fight. "Discretion is the better part of valour," the Buddha had decreed. "Better to hang ten than to hang." Dodo had reluctantly retreated, promising to take heed for once in his life.

In his mind's eye, as he squatted there in suptapadangusthasana – reclining big toe pose – his right little toe touching the back of his left ear lobe, the Buddha gazed a thousand miles into the distance, chewing over a menu for this evening. A last supper of sorts, among friends and without absent friends. He would spare a spoon in the pot for them all, as you never knew who might show.

Apart from the crew already counted, there would also be Martin, Gail and Jaia; Mike, Ziggy and Zsa Zsa, who were on their way home with a pet pig called Arnold, who followed her everywhere. If Ever Ramirez ever turned up it would be super, then there was Ozzie Bo and Rain Bo and just plain Bo. The Fox twins would come, who were pretty but also pretty peeved at being told they were as cute as foxes, since the first day they appeared in a pram. One of them was Josh. No one ever remembered the second fellow's name, so they both ended up being called Josh. Ruby would be along with her friend Terrazzo, a girl originally from Rosenallis and an expert on healing and herbs. Always great company was Nick, Gill and Magnum, John John, Jimmy, their sister Jen, Tna, Terry, Darren the philosopher and the Bun Wallis, who, as you may have guessed, was a master baker.

It was as easy to cook for a crew as a few, the Buddha chuckled to himself, as he settled into a relaxation posture, savasana, corpse pose. There, on the broad of his back, the Buddha mulled some more over the menu.

CHAPTER XVI

The Spit o' the Father

'There's smell of fresh cut grass
And it's filling up my senses
And the sun is shining down on the blossoms in the avenue
There's a buzzing fly hanging
Around the bluebells and daisies.'

Li Li was a doting aunt. Buddha had grown fond of the boy and they had formed a bond during this exodus, but he was nevertheless glad of the break to enjoy the super bowl of ramen she had prepared for him.

"You are so very lucky to be alive so," Li Li consoled him as he unashamedly slurped down the garlic-riddled ramen. After travelling up through Shimbashi, Shibuya and Shinjuku the Buddha had eventually tracked Li Li down in the district of Ikebukuro. She was beside herself with delight to greet the pair. A single, shuddering gong announced a sight for sore eyes as they came through the gates and into the courtyard carpeted in cherry blossom petals, as the fleeting festival of Hanami grasped and gasped its last breaths on the spring gusts.

"Lulu was too fond of you and running after rainbows. What good did it do her?" Li Li asked the Buddha scoldingly, as she felt entitled to. He offered no defence.

"The boy is the spit of the father, all the same," she pronounced, glancing up. Again, the Buddha thought better of mixing it; it was better to take his medicine. "I suppose the apple doesn't fall far from the tree. This boy is a very good boy."

Hearing this, the Buddha thought it best again not to make any bad apple jokes, although he couldn't help but notice Li Li's strong Japanese accent, even though she was from the midlands. He couldn't help but notice either the demeanour and manner of Lulu being echoed as Li Li cradled her nephew.

"How much longer can your luck hold out Buddha? Even though you spend so much time with those witches, you are not, after all, a black cat," Li Li teased. "Or are you?" she pondered on second thoughts.

Li Li had good cause to be vexed with him, especially now that he had effectively put her life in danger too. The resonance of the gong had not yet finished when a dove had, suddenly, flown through the open door. It had not brought best tidings. Kiyomasa was already aware of the Buddha's arrival with the boy and summoned them all to Minakami-machi in the mountains, where he continued to stalk the last dragon. He urged them to make haste, as he was certain of great cause for celebrations and needed to plan yet another Matsuri festival. The purpose of the festival was to bring the gods from their shrines to walk among the people and share in their joy on the death of the dragon.

It was three days march to Minakami. Li Li exhorted the Buddha not to delay. "This is Kiyomasa. You are but another trophy, Buddha, and you are not dealing with any Amoebae now. You will not escape his clutches and any attempt puts us all in great peril. Don't forget that you promised my sister to save the boy," she asserted, all the while in furious finger-wagging mode, lest the Buddha was in any doubts as to his priorities. She was clearly tormented.

Li Li's reference to the Amoebae was not lost on the Buddha. Only that she knew he wasn't given to fibs, much less lies, she wouldn't have believed his incredible narrow escape out of Hawaii. A pair of amphibious Amoeba assassins had set out to collect the bounty on the Buddha. The Amoeba had no backbone and even less loyalty; they were pure snakes who ran with the hare and hunted with the hound. They were ruthless. Survival at all cost was their bottom line, the bounty their only prize. These cutthroats always remained anonymous.

The Buddha and the boy had been blown off course and he was breathless when they landed at Waikiki instead of at Wailua. He had not found his feet when the first of the Amoeba moved in for the kill, as the Buddha, hands full, waded ashore in the shallows inside the reef. As the Amoeba made his move, his accomplice raced towards the Buddha, disarming him with only lei in hand and a broad grin across his face. As the murderous pair lunged at the Buddha they were plunged headlong into water without as much as a whimper, their heads gashed off a craggy outcrop only inches beneath the surface and held down by the nape of their necks until their frantic flapping ceased and they floated on the rip current face down, the crimson trickle from their cracked skulls tracing their route out to sea. The demise of the

Amoebae had been all thanks to Pulpo, who had moved so fast, you'd swear he had eight or ten pairs of hands.

"I owe you one, Pulpo," the Buddha whispered in acknowledgment of his saviour, still shuddering at the sight of the gory flotilla.

"Only one, Buddha?" Pulpo, the Sea Shepherd, replied with a guffaw, his voice rising like a tide all around. "I count two. I see you still haven't lost your knack for the art of the understatement. Don't worry about their souls, they had none. As you might say yourself, they forgot to breathe and tonight they sleep with the fishes."

Li Li had fond memories of Pulpo and could see him say those words just as the Buddha described the scene on Waikiki. "I met him once in Connemara when he stopped off to repair after a run-in with a go of Norwegians. He was mighty," Li Li recalled. Buddha did not press the matter but continued with his saga.

"Head straight for Lani's on the north shore; you should have gone there in the first place," the Sea Shepherd had said to Buddha, but he was preaching to the converted. "You can hold up for the night. Your foes are rampant; they want the boy back and you buried. The boy can sup on coconut milk and I know how much you like pineapple. I've spoken to Honu and he will post two sea turtles as sentries. They're not the swiftest but they're sound," Pulpo informed a grateful Buddha. Not one for standing on ceremony, Pulpo disappeared as suddenly as he had shown up.

Shantaram and Siddhartha the sea turtles were solid, sturdy types, but far more studious and quick-witted than their snail's pace suggested. They had for Buddha good news and bad news. The bad news was that Kamehameha's warriors, while returning from a raiding party, had discovered the pair of dead Amoeba. The King immediately knew it to be the handiwork of Pulpo, as they had had run-ins before. With this in mind, he had dispatched a brace of his finest fighters to finish off the task, rather than resorting to bounty hunters. The sea turtles had spied the two, armed to the teeth, just around the headland, where they had made camp for the night in preparation for their assault at dawn.

Kamehameha wanted the Buddha alive. It was not that he had had a change of heart, mind. It was just that, with no hair on his head harmed, Kamehameha would offer the Buddha up as human sacrifice for victory and gratitude for the safe return of the Dong's heir. He would send the boy home onboard a cargo of pineapples and the Dong would forever be in his debt. In accordance with tradition, the Buddha would be taken at sunrise and sentenced to death at sunset.

The Buddha failed to see the 'good news' side of things as set out by the seemingly nonchalant sea turtles, who were over the moon, it seemed to him, about the stay of execution. "'Get a good night's rest,'" they had advised. The necks of them, thought the Buddha, who couldn't remember another thing as he was out for the count, wrecked.

The Buddha was shattered to the point of despair when he awakened, much later, to the sight of Shantaram and Siddhartha missing. He was abandoned. With certain death his fate, his friends too would now perish. His confidence was at rock bottom and nothing – not the gentle lapping of the waves and the baby sounds in chorus from Tekisui – could do to lift him from this low ebb.

A heavy heart and heavy steps took him plodding round the headland. He had decided to accept what lay in store for him and, to save a skirmish that could hurt the child, would go quietly. To his astonishment however, as he made towards the grove, he could make out the presence of Kamehameha's finest, as if resting against the tree, their weapons stashed to one side, fire still smouldering.

These boys gave a whole new meaning to the phrase 'armed to the teeth'. Their Koa wood weapons were studded with monumental amounts of tiger shark teeth. Searing spears too, finished off with blue marlin bills. Daggers, clubs and knuckle-dusters to hand were more favoured, however, as they preferred to deal in death at close quarters. Once they got their teeth into you and saw the white in your eyes, your destiny was decided.

The Buddha was so close to them now that his early morning shadow spanned their torsos. The ferocious warriors were seemingly sound asleep, but in fact they were dead to the world, apparently sent on their way without a struggle. The only telltale sign of their demise was that their skulls had been split open on top, beneath their thick crop of hair. Killed by coconuts from the towering tree they took for refuge.

"Do you know that more people are killed each year by falling coconuts than from shark attacks? You don't read that in the papers, no. It's the odd rogue shark that gets all the bad press and gives everyone else a bad name, but not a word about the killer coconuts – they're all sweet bounty and breast milk," Pulpo lectured as he showed up at the scene. The Buddha could never tell if Pulpo was being serious or not. Before he dispatched them that evening the Sea Shepherd did confess that Shantaram and Siddhartha were scarcely shell-shocked, as he put it with a big grin, but "up to their necks" in helping to dislodge half a dozen ripe coconuts. Nature and gravity then took their course. "Not as slow as they look, those two," he added, before uncharacteristically pulling the Buddha to one side with a tug on his shoulder to whisper a request that he pass on Pulpo's best regards to Li Li.

Li Li hadn't reacted one whit to the parable of the killer coconuts or to Pulpo's overtures. Now the Buddha was certain his luck had bottomed out, as he sat naked in the steaming open air Takaragawa Onsen, finally face to face with the infamous samurai Kiyomasa, slayer of dragons and tigers and soon to add a Buddha to his list.

Normally, the Buddha would love to relax in the soothing hot springs as Hanami finally came to the mountains. Now, however, he didn't need the fleeting and fragile pink petals of the cherry blossom to remind him of the frailty of life. His great friends Lulu and Tekisui were gone. He worried too for Dodo, who was left to his own devices. As his skin softened, his heart hardened and his blood boiled. The Buddha sat there, a prisoner in the Minakami mountain onsen, as Kiyomasa bragged and blustered, his arms folded across his belly, his boasting bursting the Buddha's head. What the Buddha wouldn't give now for a lovely pair of coconuts to crack the samurai's skull.

Instead, the Buddha had to settle with staring through him and his story of how he had stalked the last dragon for days on end, up and down the Tonegawa River and the eleven waterfalls of Teriha canyon, Tekisui teasing him each morning and evening. Tekisui's lust for the icy cold waters cascading from the snow-capped peaks was his final undoing, as, even by Kiyomasa's telling, the dragon seemed to deliberately dally longer than usual when he foolishly reassumed his large dragon shape and took the waters from the Tonegawa that sunset. He was beheaded by the samurai's sword and his carcass left to perish in the riverbed. Tekisui's great bulk is still to be seen today at low water, as the rapids shoot over the dragon's back at Ryu Ga Sei.

As Kiyomasa blathered on and on, the Buddha allowed his thoughts to roam on the refreshing waters of the rampant river shooting below the onsen. He drifted on the current to the last evening in the See-Through Forest and that fabulous feast of friendship. There is nothing in the world more nourishing than true friends. They took delight in telling him that the forest was better and more commonly known as the Rainbow Forest and he had gladly stood corrected.

He had pulled out all the stops for that last supper. After considering a ratatouille bake, a spiced cashew nut paella, vegetable stew with Indian yellow dal, carrot and cucumber salad (with tofu and fresh dill dressing), he had opted instead for one of his favourites: a nut and lentil roast, perfectly suited to cooking in the oven-like conditions inside the trunk of the see-through trees, served up with rhubarb chutney and a herby potato gratin. In any event, he had been put off the idea of the vegetable stew for the moment, as the last time he had served it up on a surfari road trip it hadn't gone down so well.

"Have you got something we could dip in this?" Zulu had asked in all innocence. "Yeah, something like lamb chops," Biker clarified, in a well-planned pincer movement, much to the Buddha's dismay.

"Spuds and the Buddha, never far apart," joked Shem, who lit up the place when he had arrived with Sakineh, Erika and Gee Gee, just in time for dinner. They had drummed, danced and discussed late into the night, often hot and heavy but never out of hand. They all adjourned back to Rich's tee pee, where it seemed as though there was a thousand of them and a thousand stories told around the campfire at its centre, all squashed in but cosy nonetheless. The Buddha sent the place into convulsions and at one point it seemed that the entire tee pee would topple over, when he made the mistake in the euphoria of the evening to divulge his concepts for cooking.

A fine cut of a man for his age, the Buddha liked to sing and sway as he chopped and cooked away in the kitchen, a big fan of the showbands he confessed, much to his regret for the slagging onslaught that followed.

"Take Dickie Rock. They don't call him Dickie Rock for nothing, you know. Or Big Tom; they don't call him Big Tom for nothing either," the Buddha said, and he should have known to quit when he was ahead. Predictably, his captive audience all drew a collective breath in amused silence. "Best of them all though is Joe Dolan. It's true, there is no show like a Joe Show."

"What about the Clonaslee Show, Buddha?" piped up Seymour, who showed up in the tent out of nowhere.

"Next time I'll bring a marquee, not a tee pee," beamed Rich, realising that crowd control was now in the hands of the gods, as the Buddha admired his world-beating smile and laid-back charm.

"The real secret of good cooking," the Buddha prevailed, "is the showband recipe: 'send them home sweating and wanting just a little more.'" That observation was enough to bring the house down and it also explained the Buddha's penchant for a treble proportion of chopped red chilli in the nut and lentil roast.

A light drizzle danced on the flowers, urging them to open up a little as the dew winked a welcome to the rising sun. The tee pee people snoozed and snored, arms and legs awry. As the Buddha slipped away, there was no need for long goodbyes. He gently lifted Terrazzo's arm from across his midriff as he crept out on all fours, headfirst through the flap. Unknownst to themselves, a gang of grazing goats guzzling grass and clover played a mellow morning minuet with the bells dangling from their necks. The Buddha spared a minute to take stock of a stunning hummingbird hawk moth, as it hovered and hoovered over a patch of cowslips.

The Buddha's daydreaming in the onsen came to an abrupt end when Kiyomasa stood up in front of his face in all his glory. If it walks like a duck and looks like a duck, then it must be trouble, the Buddha thought to himself, struggling to suppress the volcano of laughter welling inside him, relishing how much Dodo would have enjoyed the moment.

Robed again, the samurai left the Buddha sitting and stewing in the hot water. Duck or no duck, the Buddha deducted that his goose was cooked. With one clap, Kiyomasa commanded his team of taiko drummers to commence. Theirs were the only instruments he would tolerate. Deemed the finest and fittest in all Japan, they took up their positions on both banks of the onsen and the bridges spanning the water, so that the deafening sound of the drums pulsated from all sides. These men were recruited from the time they were four years of age and were not allowed touch a drum until they were twelve, religiously practising in between by learning how to clap in perfect time and skip to one rhythm. On Kiyomasa's signal, they stopped.

This time there were two claps and Li Li herself arrived, surrounded by scores of servants. Kiyomasa had ordered fugu specially prepared in his honour to celebrate the death of the dragon. The samurai had not sucked a second on the first morsel of the white globefish when he keeled over. Kiyomasa died instantly from the ill-prepared poisonous puffer fish, leading to consternation throughout the household. Everyone was in a flap, it seemed to the Buddha, except Li Li, who didn't look the least bit surprised.

Amid the tumult, she sent him on his way with a strong embrace, a gentle peck on the cheek and a whisper of her fond regards to Pulpo.

As he hunkered down to refresh at Yamabiko Falls and wait for the moon to surface, the Buddha pondered the prospects of a pompous pontificator perishing at the taste of a puffer fish. But he didn't ponder for long, as he knew, with the baby Tekisui safe, what he must now do and where he must go. He dreaded the thoughts. He must make it back to the Burren and salvage what he could. Hopefully, his luck had not run out. Leaving a trail of death in his wake, he had now amassed a reputation worse than any dragon and he had not raised a finger. Now, for the first time in his life, the Buddha feared going home and the fate that awaited him.

With some time to spare before the moon changed shifts with the sun, Buddha allowed his thoughts to wander on the spray one last time, reassured by the rainbows ribboning across the cascade. Escape south to Oz, he confessed to considering. There would be the earthy scent of the Wollemi Pine, the towering silver-barked Karri and Marri forests of Boranup, captured in the sunlight and standing still. He could fashion perfectly balanced Jarrah walking poles for weary travellers like himself. He longed just once more to see the Bungle Bungle, the giants of the Kimberley, or head south along the west coast, to check out the surf in Margaret River before setting up home for the winter in a hollowed-out Red Tingle Tree in the Valley of the Giants. Along the route, he would take the chance to spend time with the Noongar, to enjoy their original thinking and six seasons.

The Buddha was peeved with himself for this pointless plotting. He might as well have strayed into Werinitj, the Devil's Place, and the sinking sands of the Pinnacles. He had been sailing close to the wind and he could not afford to get blown off course now. How he longed for September and plucking blackberries from briars beneath Ballycoolan, with Mount Leinster lurking in the background. Or to see the last of the season's tomatoes in Cremorgan, blushing fiercely for fear of being left behind. To experience the Atlantic swell in the west, sensing the offshore north-easterlies and rolling up their sleeves to meet them head-on, with the Gulf Stream warming to the idea. He knew only full well that he couldn't have his jam and eat it. The time had come to heed his own advice and keep his eye on the ball. This was not a matter of life and death; it was more important than that. He was heading for Ballyhuppahaun, come hell or high water, where he would hurl like Christy Ring.

CHAPTER XVII

Feast or a famine

'I was perched outside in the pouring rain
Trying to make myself a sail
Then I'll float to you my darling
With the evening on my tail.'

Sorley Boy put on a savage spread for the Fir Bolg when they came to connive at Dunluce Castle. The skivvies slaved away at ramming speed in the sweltering oven of a kitchen. "This is no loaves and fishes affair," the Senator indicated to Sorley Boy from the corner of his mouth. "We may not have enough for the multitudes but best keep this mob onside." They feasted over laden platters and plates, requiring creels to ferry the food and plenty from the bowels of the castle to the bellies of the Fir Bolg and their consorts.

Blood pudding sausages, red deer, stewed chickens, roast pheasant (stuffed with prunes, French style), sauced oysters, hashed hare (flavoured with nutmeg and lemon, served with onion), giblets in wine dressed with dulse and spinach, baked small game birds – woodcocks, larks, blackbirds and sparrows – in a pie, were the order of the day. There was almond cake with currants for afters, along with barrels of ale and jugs of mead to help it on its way. They would gorge as if there was no tomorrow.

Things had not quite worked out the way the Dong had planned. Zako was dead. There was no word of his son and the Buddha still at large, after strangling his beloved Lulu. He was reduced to relying on the Senator and that two-timing Sorley Boy. There would be hell to pay.

The Rainbow Travellers and Dinosaur Clans had been easily routed from Ballyhuppahaun, their reinforcements intercepted and in disarray. They had resurged from the Slieve Blooms, Strawberry Beds, Sugar Loaf, Sierras, Steppes, Siberia, the Savannah, Serengeti, Siam, Sun Dance, Soweto and Stradbally but had been quickly quashed. Now though, it was time for the denouement and the Dong was taking no chances, as too much had already gone amiss.

His foes were beaten but he wanted them destroyed – Buddha and all – and he would have to flush him out. No one could be trusted, as even Zako had proven to be feeble when push came to shove. The Dong had forged a pact with Sreng, the fiercest of the Fir Bolg, but he feared a double cross. They had agreed to return from banishment in Macedonia and to fight as allies in return for their lands.

"Go to hell or take Connacht," the Dong had commanded, laying down the law as the negotiations wavered, with the small proviso that they must first cleanse the province of the Rainbow rebels and their ilk. A hard bargain he had struck, but palms were spit and hands were shook. Just as well, as he smelled mutiny in the ranks of his regulars and militias.

"Your armies are sick and tired, though victorious. They call out for their pay and their salt," pined the Senator.

"My poor brother, lost in battle. My infant son missing and my wife not cold in the grave and they would rub salt in the wounds. Have I not given them enough? Enough heroes to bury over and over again in their ballads? Perhaps they are not worth their salt? What say you Senator, or whose side are you on? You say Lulu was strangled, but I think it was her heart that stopped. It stopped loving – she died of a broken heart." As the Dong weaved his web, the Senator was too full of fear to even flap.

"Let them eat pineapples. Give them the pineapples shipped from Hawaii, without my son on board of course. Let them eat pineapples. Pineapples don't grow on trees you know," the Dong hollered. The Senator was still not sure if he was serious and didn't know which way to look. Had the Dong completely lost it? They'll lynch me if I propose pineapples, the Senator thought, before considering it best to keep it to himself and to take that plan with a pinch of salt.

With that much settled, the Dong had another task for the Senator. It was to arrange a parley at Dunluce Castle in the north. Sorley Boy, the local chief, would comply or die.

"Sit down the Fir Bolg and fete them some more, as their kin are set to join the fray from Scotland. Make sure their heads and hearts are not turned, as there is talk of rapprochement between them and the feckin' Fomorians. Those lugs will get what's coming to them, and they only thinking of one thing – getting into bed with the Rainbow Travellers, that band of witches and the Buddha."

The Fomorians had some old scores to settle with both the Fir Bolg and the Dong and, even as the King spoke, they were making their way for Antrim. The Dong was not entirely wrong either when he suspected that the Fomorians had a soft spot for the witches, which may have made them weak at the knees but forged them as sturdy steel in battle.

"Break open the war chest," the King directed, the Senator too shocked to sound protest. "I have decided to finish this once and for all; we will unleash the Dogs of War." Now the Senator had no doubts at all: the Dong had lost it, but he was loathe to even think the thought for more than a moment, in case the King would read his mind. This war would now bankrupt the country, with not a coin left in their coffers.

"Kill 'em all! Kill 'em all! That will be your instructions to the mercenaries at Dunluce. We will embrace them as a third force to our ranks to fight alongside our armies and the Fir Bolg as one. The black, three-leaf shamrock will be our flag, 'Death from Above' our motto and our promise. Never before in the history of mankind will there have been so much death and we will deliver it from above as they cower down for mercy."

The Dong delivered his instructions with a venom that scared the living daylights out of the Senator. He was paralysed with fear and unable to breathe a word of objection. Best just to obey, he decided meekly. He would meet with the leaders of the soldiers of fortune – Johnny the Fox, Jimmy the Weed and Joe Milis – along with the Fir Bolg at Dunluce. Destiny was decided; no one would escape and no one would survive. The mercenaries, if paid high enough a price, would see to that and a high price would be paid. 'Death from Above'.

It was with no small degree of relief that the Senator pressed up through the Lakelands as he made for Dunluce. Relief that his own hide was still intact and that he had lied to the Dong about the deaths of Lulu and Zako. This confirmed his long-held view that sometimes it was best to lie for the greater good. Lulu was poisoned – not even the chief court physician had the stomach to tell that to the King.

Buddha the Strangler had a better ring. As for Zako, well, who knows what snapped there. Killed in a skirmish with vagabonds in Świętokrzyski was the official explanation, the ignominy of such a dishonourable death not at all pleasing the Dong. Much less, then, did he need to know the truth, the Senator deduced. By the time Zako had gotten to the Tatra Mountains to ensure that the populace had rounded on the witches, he need not have bothered. With the healing waters of the Black Pond contaminated and children dying in their dozens, the finger of blame soon pointed at the witches, just as the Dong had planned.

As the mounds of little limp bodies piled up on the pyres, so too mounted the desire for recrimination and retribution. Before long, a frenzy for revenge forced the witches to abandon the meadows and they took refuge in the forests and caves. Though some made good their escape through the Sea Eye, thousands of others, once captured, didn't stand a prayer and were strung up on the spot or burned screaming at the stake. A pall of smoke and the stench of despair filled the air in a persecution that was to last a further 300 years, long after the poisonous plague that struck down the children had passed.

As he viewed the cursed work from a vantage along Liliowe Pass, Zako thought back to his boyhood and the burning butterfly. Overcome with remorse, he dismissed his contingent and, lightheaded, went to lie down across the mountain ridge. Frozen overnight, he was never awoken and his shape can still be made out on a clear view as the 'sleeping knight', to this very day. He gives his name to the town below in the valley, Zakopane.

There was a tumultuous clatter as Leper, the most vicious of the mercenaries, full of liquor, made a drive at the buxom servant in the kitchen at Dunluce. Displaying some deft footwork, which belied her full figure, the girl sidestepped her lecherous pursuer, the lout crashing full square against the gable wall, which crumbled under his brute force and bulk.

With him into the brine went a good-sized section of the kitchen, a hapless serf Leper had clung to in vain to steady himself, two live sheep, a big furry ball of a cat (which had a head on it like an owl), assorted pots and pans, culinary accoutrements and three casks of ale. The girl who had been the centre of his desire was left perched precariously on the edge, looking out onto the unforgiving North Atlantic as it lashed against the stone, continuing its relentless assault on the castle's craggy outcrop.

Such was the feasting and festivities back at the banquet that no one even missed the man. Coin had been exchanged, a king's ransom paid and the Dogs of War would delight in doing the Dong's bidding and kill them all. This would be the end of the Rainbow and, to the victors, the crock of gold.

Elsewhere however, the Fomorians had other plans. Led by Bres, on the instructions of their leader Balor (who stayed behind to rally the tribes, clans and witches for their last stand west of the Shannon) the Fomorians hatched a plan to ambush the high command of the Fir Bolg, the Soldiers of Fortune and the Senator himself. Although grossly outnumbered on the battlefield, Balor figured that if they could surprise and catch the Fir Bolg chiefs and the war-mongering mercenary moguls off-guard, there was a glimmer of hope.

The Fomorians' fittest and finest commandos hugged the Antrim coastline as they clung to darkness, past Carrickfergus, Carnlough, Cushendall, Cushendun and Carrick-a-Rede, where they fashioned a rope bridge and secured their supplies. From here, they were within striking distance of Dunluce. Balor had struck a deal with Sorley Boy that he would signal the departure of the Dong's allies, once he had gotten them nicely sizzled so as they could be set upon with ease.

For whatever reason, fear or favour, Sorley Boy failed in his side of the deal, in what became known as the infamous Dunluce double-cross. Instead, he prematurely signalled to the Fomorians, luring them from their hideout. When they got within an asses bawl of Dunluce, he sent a second message that it was a false alarm and that they should hold up on the rocks just south of Benbane Head and await his nod. Perishing outside in the frost, Sorley Boy had his servant girls move among the Fomorians and ply them with whiskey, mellow as honey, distilled from the nearby River Bush.

Giants of men, the Fomorians didn't know when they'd had enough. As their foe fled in the night without a hand being raised, the Fomorians slept soundly and in their slumber their friends and families perished. It is of much dispute to this day as to whether the Fomorians falling asleep on the job was the defining moment in this epic struggle. Whether it was for weeks or months is immaterial now as, by the time they sobered up, too many days and lives had been lost. So long had the Fomorians lay hungover and sitting among the rocks on their fat arses that they wore the basalt formations slippery smooth as you see them today – formations known locally as the Giant's Causeway.

By the time the Buddha got back to Ballyhuppahaun the place was levelled. He followed the scent of death and destruction back over the bogs, across the Shannon and into the west. A blaze he had picked out from the height of the Stoney Man back in the Slieve Blooms (where you could see unhindered in all directions for three hundred miles) was edging closer and looking more ominous now. He had even come to hope that the pyre was merely piled high with parchments and books that the Dong had pledged to burn. This was a bonfire of bodies however, just as he had feared. So high did it blaze that it could be seen from Malin to Mizen. It was as if Katla itself had erupted again. The Buddha later learned that it was these flames that sprung Dodo from Donegal in a fit of rage.

With a pain in the pit of his stomach, the Buddha searched every corner of Connacht for Dodo but in despair. A pair of distraught witches, taking refuge by the roadside at Tulla, told the Buddha that they had last seen Dodo being hunted down by the Dogs of War, Johnny the Fox and Jimmy the Weed, near Kilfenora. The Buddha never found Dodo or heard tell of him again. Dodo wasn't gone for good; he was gone forever.

The Dong's promise had not been an idle one. His harrowing words came back to haunt the Buddha: "Wars need soldiers and soldiers need wars. There is a world of difference in not being afraid to die and not being afraid to kill." There was no defence for what happened here. These were no mean soldiers. These were soldiers of fortune and their destiny was death. They were hardened veterans of previous campaigns. They dealt in death on the Somme, Sri Lanka, Sinai, Saigon, Somalia, Srebrenica, Son My, Sabra, Suvla, Salamanca, Shankill, Sarajevo, Shatila, Salonica, Katyn, Khmer, Khartoum, Kabul, Kandahar, Kigali, Kosovo, Berlin, Biafra, Batan,

Bogside, Bilatserkva, Badajoz and Omagh. These men were no strangers to terror, torture and torment.

Now they plied their handiwork as they pillaged and raped across Connacht, collecting body parts as souvenirs on the battlefield of the Burren, moving amidst their latest masterpiece.

By the time the Buddha made it back to the Burren all was lost, save for stragglers and an assortment of wiry and wily survivors. Desperation and defeat had made way for forlorn and abject hopelessness. It was easy talking to the last of the Dinosaur Clans and Rainbow Tribes now. The Dong had decreed among the ranks that he wanted the war finished swiftly – by Samhain – and he would celebrate their triumph with a victory march through the White Cities of Babylon and the Shadowlands to mark his birthday on November 15th.

So much blood had been spilled that even the peaceful puffins forsake the cliffs, their black beaks for evermore spattered in gore. They sought sanctuary in the open sea, returning only once a year to hatch a solitary egg on the rocks before flocking once more to the expanse of the ocean. So too for the clans and tribes: there would be once final chance, one last stand for survival.

The Buddha would have to reveal the most ancient secret of the Rainbow Travellers and call on the spirit of the dragons and the intervention of the Tuatha Dé Danann, not for support but for some succour, which they would not refuse to a needy traveller.

On the eve of Samhain, the Buddha summoned a final gathering. As he beheld from the centre of the circle the hundreds and thousands of famished faces, there was little that needed to be said, no persuading that needed to be done. Since beyond time, he told them, those with a good heart and those who believed it was possible had travelled freely and majestically at will, riding on the rainbow as it bridges the gap between the sun and the moon. These were the true Rainbow Travellers. This is why, he explained, that he always waited for the dawn or departed in the evening when the sun and moon hung out together and the rainbow paid them a visit.

With their hearts in the right place and trusting in the power of the rainbow, the tribes could now decide, once they did not look back, to come and go overnight. The Buddha would lead them to the end of the rainbow, which would empower their spirit to change. They would have to forego their earthly form, as had been agreed with the Tuatha Dé Danann, and would morph as mushrooms to move freely through the plains and forests ever after. They would then be allowed to gather in great numbers at this time each year to mark their passing from one life to the next.

And so it came to pass that mushrooms were formed. Made up of all the colours of the rainbow, all shapes and sizes, all types, creeds and colours, as the last survivors of the tribes took their chances to live a magical life of mystery as mushrooms. One moment there and gone the next on the dawn, at dusk and with the dew. As with the best of plans, there were infiltrators and collaborators, spies within, their hearts poisoned with greed and so, as no life runs smooth, there are poison mushrooms.

Getting the bulk of what remained of the Dinosaur Clans to safety was going to be a much bigger problem but the Buddha was at his best under pressure and knew exactly what to do. For years, he had been aware that the many of the dragons were desperate to abandon what they viewed as the anodyne life of a dragonfly for something a little more adventurous. It also required a leap of faith on behalf of the Dinosaur Clans, albeit that the alternative was absolute extinction, as the Dong set about his finishing moves.

The biggest and bravest of the Brontosaurus clan, including Ballykelly, Ballyadams, Balbriggan, Ballaghadereen, Ballydehop and Ballina, volunteered to stay behind, stand fast and slow down the final assault so as to buy the others some time. They fell where they stood, with their strong arching backs, one stacked upon another, and their stony grey skin forming the rugged mounds that shape and stand out in the Burren to this day. Unflinching as they faltered, they nevertheless wept as their friends and families made good their escape, the salt drops from their eyes burning crevices in the soil from where, in spring, sprouted dazzling flowers found nowhere else in the world. The bee orchid, birds-nest orchid, bloody crane's bill, dog violet and spring gentian mark their graves and the spot where they perished.

As bloody extinction marched their way, the remainder of the Dinosaur Clans, who not long before had roamed and ruled the earth, had now been run to ground and run into the ground. As the Dong's forces saw it, the tribes had disappeared in disarray and clans would die at the end of the world as they forced them over the edge of the earth at the Cliffs of Moher.

As the final assault came at dawn, the moon hung over the horizon and the sun peered out through the hills. A weak but willing hazy rainbow spanned the ocean and the land as the daylight sparkled through the Atlantic spray. One by one, the clans when toppled, tripped or tipped over the top of the cliffs and plunged towards the waves, in what should have been certain death. As they screamed, roared and bellowed, the dragons in the form of the dragonflies flew into their open mouths and straight, deep down to their bellies, breaking their fall and fetching them into the sea as giants of the ocean. That is how whales were born. The clans had paid a high price for their survival but it beat extinction all the same.

For his part, the Buddha witnessed the organised chaos with some small sense of nervous satisfaction, constantly clinging to the hope that in any moment he might spot Dodo emerging from out of the melee. He scanned through the consternation too for his great friends the witches – Grażyna, Gemma, Gráinne, Gill and the others – but there was no sign or sight of them.

His heart broken, the Buddha turned for a split second to survey the shore and see how fared the clans as they set about cheating death for a second chance. In a blink, however, the Buddha was gone. It was never truly known if he had jumped or was shoved head-first down the face of the cliffs before perhaps being swallowed in the foam.

Scattered to the seven seas, the clans roam the oceans deep and still. They cry out and sing their hymn of hardship, as a warning to all and any that will listen. Still hunted in the deep, they voice their sad song for their saviour and sometimes, when there is sun and moon and rainbow in the sky, they climb out of the water, daring one last look for – one fleeting glimpse of – the Buddha of Ballyhuppahaun.

The Mazury Breaks

'When the moon is in the Seventh House
And Jupiter aligns with Mars
Then peace will guide the planets
And love will steer the stars.'

For years and for what seemed like forever, these friends have been making this annual pilgrimage to Mazury. Making way for the lightning storm that threatens the evening on Lake Śniardwy, they leave Skorupki in their wake and, with sails full-on, make for the shelter of Sowi Róg.

Aboard three yachts, this motley crew anchor up, bows first tethered to sturdy birch and oak. The storks have left for Africa but in September, they merely swap places with the mushrooms carpeting the primeval forests. The bison, though, not afraid of frost, continue to explore deep behind the woods along the marshes of the Biebrza.

Riding on the Galway Hooker, Galician Girl and Fremantle are our captain Mirek, a stickler for safety (coming here since childhood, he knows the place like the back of his hand and is widely regarded wherever we go) and Hapel, a happy-go-lucky bulk of a man and a master cook (his Chiapas dish is to die for).

Also on the crew, Stefan is extremely resourceful, has a delicious honey vodka recipe and you always feel safe when he's around, while Bodzio is solid out and a great photographer. Wujek, meanwhile, is a much-revered expert on wild mushrooms; Edek – a cigar smoking raconteur; Elek, our intrepid interpreter-in-chief; and the entertainers Mariusz and Olek, for whom there is not a chord or a chorus born yet than can evade them.

Spoko, the happy-go-lucky one, is a perfect foil for the pensive poet Tadzio. Then there's me: Johnny Renko, a stowaway, declared lost at sea after going overboard.

With the fire lit, the preparations are soon followed by a singsong soaked in companionship, steeped in tradition and later perhaps to be saturated in vodka. A big black pan is also blazing away, singing and spitting its own tune to the sound of a tasty mushroom mix with crispy fried bread for a sailor's supper. There are chanterelle, parasol, brown birch bolette, slippery jack, and the much sought after and best of all: penny bun.

"Can you eat this one?" asks the stray Johnny Renko, holding up a long, funny-looking fungus by the stalk for an expert opinion.

"You can eat all mushrooms," instructs the captain Mirek, before pausing and adding, "But some of them, only once."

Uproar around the fire; shouts of 'Na Zdrowie!' on breaths hanging in the cool air as the Luxusowa potato vodka does its rounds. The lake is still now after the downpour and the sun about beaten, sitting like an orange ball in a childish crayon drawing, shimmering, clinging to the water's edge, with the moon now daring to show its face out of the woods. A rainbow appears from nowhere to make a false promise, of no more rain.

This trip has only started. Olek wastes no time and seizes the moment, banging out the familiar opening chords, an invitation for all to join in his shanty.

"So fare thee well, my own true love
When I return united we will be
It's not the leaving of Liverpool that's grieving me
But my darling when I think of thee."

History always repeats itself;
first, as tragedy, then as farce.

Karl Marx

Soundtrack

The Buddha of Ballyhuppahaun
The Enchanted Place

Those Were the Days
Mary Hopkins and Sundance

Brothers
Brand New

Mursheen Durkin
Johnny McEvoy

Love and Only Love
Neil Young and Crazy Horse

An Poc ar Buile
Seán O Sé (to an arrangement by Seán O Riada)

I Am The Highway
Audioslave

Psycho Killer
Talking Heads

All Along the Watchtower
Bob Dylan/The Jimi Hendrix Experience

A Rainy Night In Soho
The Pogues

Man In The Mirror
Michael Jackson

Earth Song
Michael Jackson

Sit Down
James

Free Fallin'
Tom Petty and the Heartbreakers

Dancing in the Moonlight
Thin Lizzy

(I Never Promised You) A Rose Garden
Lynn Anderson

The Garden Song
Arlo Guthrie

Fallin' and Flyin'
Jeff Bridges ('Crazy Heart' OST)

Whatever You Say, Say Nothing
Colum Sands/Brendan Nolan

And the Band Played Waltzing Matilda
Eric Bogle

The Wild Side of Life
Hank Thompson/Status Quo

Trouble with a Capital 'T'
Horslips

Don't Go
Hothouse Flowers

Candy
Paolo Nutini

Aquarius/Let the Sunshine In
The 5th Dimension (from the musical *Hair*)

Leaving of Liverpool
The Dubliners

Sources and Acknowledgments

Gulliver's Travels
Jonathan Swift

Animal Farm
George Orwell

Henry IV
William Shakespeare

Zen Flesh, Zen Bones
compiled by Paul Reps
and Nyogen Senzaki

The Holy Bible
(standard editions)

A Bright Shining Lie
Neil Sheehan

The Backyards of Heaven
eds. John Ennis and
Stephanie McKenzie

The Berlin Wall Cafe
Paul Durcan

The Way of the Surfer: Living it,
1935 to Tomorrow
Drew Kampion

Dinosaurs
Steve Brusatte
and Michael Benton

Jim's Kitchen
Jim Tynan

Jim's Kitchen 2
Jim Tynan

The Blazing Salads Cookbook
Lorraine Fitzmaurice
Joe Fitzmaurice
and Pamela Fitzmaurice

A Dictionary of Hiberno-English:
The Irish Use of English
Terence Patrick Dolan

A Dictionary of Celtic Myth and Legend
Miranda J. Green

Focloir Gaedilge agus Bearla:
An Irish-English Dictionary
Fr Patrick S Dineen

Irish Place Names
P W Joyce

Animals of Ireland
Gordon D'Arcy

Laois Society for the Prevention
of Cruelty to Animals

Penguin Encyclopaedia
ed. David Crystal

Collins Gem Birds: The Quick
and Easy Spotter's Guide
Jim Flegg

A World Without Bees
Allison Benjamin
and Brian McCallum

Bladma – Walks of Discovery
in the Slieve Bloom
Thomas P Joyce

Mushrooms
Roger Phillips

Mazury – Four Seasons
Waldemar Bzura

An Taisce

The Surf Experience
Lagos, Portugal

Escola Carioca de Surf
Rio de Janeiro, Brazil

National Trust
Dunluce Castle, County Antrim

Pinnacles Interpretative Centre
Western Australia

Meiji Jingu Shinto Shrine
Tokyo, Japan

American Museum of
Natural History
New York

Waimea Bay Folk Park
O'Ahu Island, Hawaii

Official Road Atlas, Ireland
Ordnance Survey Ireland- Ordnance
Survey Northern Ireland

*On the Portrait of Two Beautiful
Young People*
Gerard Manley Hopkins

Christy Ring
Professor Seán Ó Tuama

Cool Hand Luke
Donn Pearce

*Favourite Irish Names for Children:
The Top 200*
Laurence Flanagan

Roadtrips, great conversations
with friends, train journeys,
bus stops, house parties and,
of course, my parents,
Paddy and Nan

Translations

Galician and Spanish – Xan Guitan
Polish – Grażyna Rekosiewicz
Japanese – Pat Ryan

If you enjoyed this book why not pass it on to someone else you think would like it. If you like it so much then please tell others about it.